orphan train girl

orphan train girl

The Young Readers' Edition of *Orphan Train*

Christina Baker Kline

with Sarah Thomson

HARPER

An Imprint of HarperCollinsPublishers

Orphan Train Girl
Copyright © 2017 by Christina Baker Kline
All rights reserved. Printed in the United States of America.

Library of Congress Control Number: 2016961160
ISBN 978-0-06-244594-0 (trade bdg.)

Typography by David Curtis
17 18 19 20 21 PC/LSCH 10 9 8 7 6 5 4 3 2 1
❖
First Edition

≈

To

Christina Looper Baker,

who handed me the thread,

and

Carole Robertson Kline,

who gave me the cloth

≈

orphan train girl

Chapter One

"Well," Jack's mom says from the driver's seat. "This is it."

Molly, sitting next to Jack in the backseat of the car, eyes the house. Three full stories. More windows than she can count. Carved curlicues around the roof. The white paint is fresh and gleaming.

This is the house where Jack's mom works for a rich old lady. And now Molly is—maybe—going to work for that rich old lady too. All because she stole a book.

Well, she didn't actually steal it. Although it's true she was going to.

Molly had been in the Spruce Harbor Public Library, on her knees in the fiction section with three copies of *The Secret Garden* on the shelf in front of her. She'd pulled all three copies off the shelf. Put the hardcover back. Then the newer paperback too. The one she kept was old and dog-eared, the cover missing a corner, the yellowed pages beginning to come loose from the cheap binding. She figured nobody would miss it, and she slipped it into her backpack.

But when Molly put the backpack over her shoulders and stood up, the librarian, Mrs. LeBlanc, swooped down on her like a homing pigeon. She called Ralph and Dina, Molly's foster parents. Dina hit the roof. Molly had way too many problems, she said. She never signed up for this, she said.

Ralph calmed her down and called Lori, Molly's social worker.

"Why in the world would you try to steal an old book?" Lori asked Molly.

"I don't know," Molly said. But that wasn't entirely true. *The Secret Garden* is all about a girl who has to leave her home and travel to a cold, rainy place where nobody wants her. A girl who scowls and sulks and says horrible things and still ends up with a home—a mansion, actually—and a family.

Lori came up with a plan for Molly to do twenty hours of community service. Dina grudgingly agreed that Molly could stay, as long as she finished her hours.

And Jack—who is the best friend Molly's ever had—heard his mom grumbling about needing to help Mrs.

Daly clean out her attic, and came up with the idea for Molly to do it instead. *If* Mrs. Daly likes Molly. *If* she says yes.

Molly thinks it might have been simpler just to let Dina kick her out.

"Okay," Jack says quickly. "Here's the deal. Mrs. Daly's okay for an old lady, but kind of . . . old-fashioned."

His mom pivots to look at Molly. "What Jack means is, you need to mind your manners. Don't slouch. Say please and thank you."

"What I mean is, she's kind of uptight," Jack says.

"How old is she again?" Molly mumbles.

"I don't know. Pretty old."

"Come on, you two," his mom says. "Might as well get this over with." She gets out of the car and heads up the walk toward the house.

Molly is suddenly nervous. She looks down at her too-big pink blouse and attempts to tuck it into her skirt. The blouse is Dina's; she insisted Molly borrow it, saying it would be disrespectful to Mrs. Daly to wear her usual black T-shirt over black jeans over worn-out black tennis shoes. "Maybe if you look a little more respectable, Mrs. Daly will overlook that blue streak in your hair," Dina said.

Jack opens his car door, then hesitates. He leans toward Molly. "Listen. Mom didn't tell her about you stealing the book."

Molly twitches in her seat. "She didn't?"

"No. Just that you have to do a community service project. She thinks it's for school, like everybody has to do one," he says. "Got it?" Then he bounds out of the car and waits for Molly on the driveway.

Molly slides out more slowly. So this rich lady doesn't know that Molly is a thief. That's good—right?

Maybe. Maybe not. Maybe it means that Mrs. Daly will expect Molly to be what she definitely isn't—just like every other kid.

Gloomily, Molly follows Jack up the walk. It's one of those rare days when spring in Maine actually feels like spring, but even the warm April sun doesn't help her mood.

"Just nod and smile. That's what I do when I have to talk to her," Jack whispers as they climb the porch steps.

Molly feels like she is shrinking inside herself, getting smaller with each step as she follows Jack's mom inside and down a long hall. She tugs at the collar of the stupid pink blouse, thinking about the scene in *The Secret Garden* when Mary Lennox arrived at Misselthwaite Manor. When Mary got there, her uncle insisted that she get rid of all her dark clothes. "I won't have a child dressed in black, wandering about like a lost soul," he said. Molly feels like a fake in this outfit, and a bad fake at that. When was the last time she wore something pink? Or a blouse with a collar?

At the end of the hallway is a closed door. Jack's mom pauses before it and knocks softly. "Vivian?" She opens the door a crack. "All right for us to come in?"

Molly hears the faint reply beyond the door: "Why, certainly." Jack's mom opens the door wider, and Molly and Jack follow her into a large sunny living room. The wide windows are filled with the bright, restless blue of the sea. Sitting in a red wingback chair, wearing a snug cream-colored sweater that looks as soft as a kitten's fur, is an old lady. *The* old lady. The one who owns this giant house.

"Good morning," the old lady says.

"Good morning," Jack's mom says. "Vivian, you know my son, Jack."

He lifts his hand in a small wave. "Nice to see you, Mrs. Daly."

"And this is the girl I told you about. Molly Ayer." She gestures at Molly to step forward.

"Molly, this is Mrs. Daly," she says.

Nod and smile, Molly thinks. She nods and smiles and holds out her hand for Mrs. Daly to take. The old woman's hand is dry and cool. "Nice to meet you, Molly," she says.

"All right, then. I have some things to do in the kitchen," Jack's mother says. "Jack, why don't you come with me?"

"Can't I stay and—"

"I could use some help." Jack trails after his mother, casting a glance back at Molly that is probably meant to be encouraging.

Now Molly and Mrs. Daly are alone.

Mrs. Daly leans forward a little in her chair. She looks at Molly with interest.

Molly fights an urge to start babbling. She'd like to explain to Mrs. Daly that Jack came up with this terrible idea and then asked his mom. Although Molly doesn't know that much about real moms—moms who actually take care of their kids—she can tell that his mom doesn't say no to Jack, not much, not when it's something he really wants. And so Molly's here.

But now that Mrs. Daly has seen Molly, has seen the blue streak in her dark hair and the look on her face (Molly's trying not to have that look on her face, but it's there, she can feel it), they can all quit pretending that Molly is the kind of kid who does community service in people's attics. And she can just go. Like always.

"How on earth do you achieve that effect—the blue

stripe?" Mrs. Daly asks. She reaches up and brushes the hair at her own temple.

Smile and nod. But Mrs. Daly has asked her a question, so Molly has to answer: "Um . . . I separated out this one part and bleached it. Then I went back and dyed it blue."

"How did you learn to do it?"

"I saw a video on YouTube."

"YouTube?"

"On the internet?"

"Ah." Mrs. Daly lifts her chin. "The computer. I'm too old for such fads."

Molly blinks again. This old lady doesn't have a computer? She's never heard of YouTube?

Mrs. Daly leans back in her chair. "Excuse my bluntness, but at my age there's no point beating around the bush. Your hair . . . and your fingernails . . ." Molly glances down at her fingernails. She left most of her thrift store rings at home, but she kind of forgot about the chipped black polish. "You borrowed that blouse, I assume?"

"Uh . . ."

"You needn't have bothered. It doesn't suit you." She waves a hand, which Molly takes to mean that she can sit down. She picks a matching armchair across from Mrs. Daly and perches on the edge of the seat cushion.

"By the way, you can call me Vivian. I never liked 'Mrs. Daly.' My husband is dead, you know."

Molly nods, a little surprised at how blunt the old woman is. "I'm sorry."

"No need to be sorry. It was eight years ago. Anyway, I am in my nineties. Not many people I once knew are still alive."

Molly isn't sure what she is supposed to say to this. *Sorry*, again? Or *of course not*? Maybe *wow*? She just nods once more and makes a mental note to tell Jack that Mrs. Daly—Vivian?—is close to a century old! She wouldn't have guessed, but then she hasn't known many elderly people to compare. The only grandmother she can remember died of cancer when Molly was three.

"Terry tells me you're in foster care," Vivian says. "Are you an orphan?"

Molly lets her gaze slide from Vivian's face to the bright sunlight and shimmering water on the other side of the windows. "My mom's alive. But yes, I call myself an orphan."

"Why?" Vivian doesn't sound as if she feels particularly sorry for Molly. Or horrified. Or weirdly intrigued, the way people can be when they find out about Molly's family.

Molly's memories of her mother are a little hazy. When she thinks back, she can recall the smell of their trailer, mildew and cigarette smoke, the way the TV seemed to be on all the time. She remembers pulling open the refrigerator door when it was still big and heavy to her, and rummaging inside to find things to eat—cold hot dogs, maybe some leftover pizza. She'd do that whenever her mother was at work. And sometimes even when she was home.

"I think if you don't have parents who take care of you, you can call yourself whatever you want," Molly says.

There is a pause. Then Vivian says, "Fair enough. Tell me about yourself."

Molly has lived in Maine her entire life. She's never even crossed the state line. She remembers bits and pieces of when she was a little kid on the reservation on Indian Island—the community center with pickups parked all around, Sockalexis Bingo Palace, St. Anne's Church. She remembers the cornhusk doll her dad gave her with black yarn hair and moccasins and a long fringed dress that she kept on a shelf in her room. The truth is, she would've preferred a Barbie, like the ones donated by charities and doled out at the community center around Christmas. (They were never the popular ones like Beauty Queen Barbie or Cinderella Barbie. Instead they were the kind you find on clearance at Walmart—Hot Rod Barbie, Jungle Barbie.)

But Vivian doesn't want to hear about toys. Where should Molly start? She knows by now that people don't want to hear everything. There's a lot they'd rather not know, and a lot she'd rather not tell.

"Well." She picks a bit of nail polish off one finger. "I'm a Penobscot Indian on my father's side. When I was young, we lived on a reservation near Old Town."

She tells the rest of the story in a few sentences—her mom and dad couldn't take care of her, so she ended up with Ralph and Dina. She doesn't mention the car crash that killed her father, how her mom got worse and worse after he died until the caseworker stepped in. There weren't any foster families on the reservation who could take her, so she ended up getting shuffled around before landing with Ralph and Dina.

"Terry tells me you were assigned some kind of community service project," Vivian says.

Terry? Oh! Molly realizes. Jack's mom.

"And she came up with the brilliant idea for you to help clean out my attic. Seems like a bad bargain for you. There's nothing you'd rather do?"

Molly shrugs again. "I like organizing things."

"Then you are even stranger than you appear," Vivian says with a smile. Normally Molly would be offended, but for some reason she isn't. Is it because there's nothing in Vivian's voice to show that she thinks *strange* is the same thing as *bad*? Not like the girls at school, the way they look at Molly and whisper *"Weird."* Vivian only seems amused by the idea of a sixth grader who likes to tidy things.

Leaning forward in her chair, Vivian says, "I'll tell you something. By your definition I'm an orphan, too. So we have that in common."

Molly isn't sure how to answer. She's never met a grown-up who talks about being an orphan. Don't you have to be a kid to be an orphan? But she has to admit she's curious. "Your parents . . ." she asks hesitantly, watching Vivian's face carefully for a sign that she's saying the wrong thing. "They didn't take care of you?"

"They tried. There was a fire. . . ." Vivian shakes her head. "It was all so long ago, I barely remember."

NIAMH
NEW YORK CITY, 1929

Niamh was seven years old when her family took a berth on a ship called the *Agnes Pauline*, bound for Ellis Island. As Niamh stood on the lower deck outside the dark, cramped rooms, watching the oily water churn beneath the ship, her spirits filled with hope.

People from their village in County Galway were

always fleeing to America. In Ireland, potatoes rotted in the fields, and children cried from hunger. Many young men in their village went off to fight the British. Some came back wounded or grimly silent. Some didn't come back at all.

But in America, people said, there were oranges the size of potatoes, fields of grain waving under sunny skies, houses with water running from faucets and even electric lights. Niamh wasn't sure all that was true, but she hoped they would at least find a better life, once they arrived.

What they found were the grimy streets of lower Manhattan, a dishwashing job for Da at a pub, and a small apartment on Elizabeth Street for ten dollars a month. There was a bedroom for Niamh and her brothers and sister, an even smaller one for Mam and Da, a kitchen, and a parlor. There was, indeed, a weak electric light that Niamh could pull on with a chain, and a small, stained sink where cold water ran from a faucet. Outside in the hall there was a toilet, one they shared with their neighbors downstairs, an elderly German couple called the Schatzmans.

Da's paycheck from the pub was barely enough to feed all four children, and Ma seemed listless much of the time. And it was hard to get used to the great crowds of people, all speaking different languages. Surely there

were more people on Elizabeth Street than in their
entire village back in Ireland. Some of them twisted up
their faces or spat in disgust as soon as Niamh opened
her mouth and her Irish voice tumbled out.

Even with all of this, she felt hope. It was a chance
for a new beginning.

Chapter Two

MOLLY
SPRUCE HARBOR, MAINE, PRESENT DAY

The next Monday, after school, Terry leads the way to the third floor. Vivian moves slowly behind her. Molly brings up the rear.

She still can't get over the size of the house. Fourteen rooms! For one person! In one of Molly's past foster homes, there were four rooms for seven people; three were kids younger than Molly. She'd been told on the first day it would be her job to look after them.

She'd lasted a month at that place.

In Molly's hands are the supplies Terry gave her downstairs—a slippery stack of white garbage bags, a small knife with a plastic handle and a serrated edge, and a notebook with a pen clipped to it. Now Terry reaches the top of the stairs and pauses. "Yikes! Where to start, Vivi?" she asks.

Vivian reaches the top step, clutching the banister. She's wearing another expensive-looking sweater, gray this time, and a silver necklace with an odd little charm on it.

Standing behind her, Molly peers around. Floor to ceiling, the attic is packed with cardboard boxes. Overhead, pink insulation peeks out between rafters. The only open area is around the narrow windows that let in slivers of natural light and a view of the bay outside.

In one corner Molly spies a long clothes rack covered with a plastic zippered case. Several large cedar chests—how did anyone ever get them up the stairs?—are lined up against one wall, next to a stack of steamer trunks.

Vivian trails her fingertips along some bulging old cardboard boxes. Molly can make out a few labels: *The store, 1960. The Nielsens.*

"I suppose this is why people have children, isn't it?" Vivian murmurs. "So somebody will care about the stuff they leave behind."

Molly tugs her phone out of her pocket and looks at the time. 4:15. She's supposed to stay until six today, and then come back for two hours twice a week after school, and two hours on Saturday too, until the attic is finished or she's done her twenty hours. Whichever comes first.

Vivian appears to be in no hurry to get started.

"It'll be good to clear all this stuff out, Vivi," Terry is saying. "I'm going to do some laundry. Call if you need me!" She nods to Molly and scuttles down the stairs.

15

"You look much more like yourself today," Vivian says when Terry is gone, motioning toward Molly's black T-shirt. Molly doesn't know how to respond, so she heads for a window and pulls it open a crack. The attic is stuffy. "How long have all these boxes been here?" she asks.

"I haven't touched anything since we moved in," Vivian says. "That was twenty years ago."

Molly peers at a box close to her. The label says *Valuables*. How valuable could the stuff be, she wonders, if Vivian hasn't needed it in all this time?

"Were you ever tempted just to toss it all in a Dumpster?" she asks. From the sharp look Vivian turns on Molly, she realizes maybe she should think before saying the first thing that pops into her head.

But—twenty years! Vivian's had this stuff for longer than Molly has been alive. And she's never even looked at it! Tossing it all into a Dumpster doesn't seem like such an unreasonable idea. Plus it would make her job a whole lot easier.

But as Lori, her social worker, reminds her, you can usually find *something* good about wherever you are. While Molly waits for Vivian to tell her what to do, she tries to come up with a list of the things that are good, or at least not bad, about being in this attic.

One, she won't be in trouble with the library

anymore for stealing the book.

Two, she might get to stay with Ralph and Dina. Sure, Dina doesn't like her much—that's pretty obvious. It was Ralph who wanted to take in a foster kid in the first place. Still, at their house she's got a bedroom to herself, and the fridge is full of food, and she has her own cell phone, even if Jack's the only person who ever calls. It could be a lot worse.

Three, if you must spend twenty hours in an attic in Maine, spring is the best time of year to do it.

Four, Vivian is ancient, but she doesn't seem to be senile.

Five—who knows? Maybe there will actually be something interesting in one of these boxes.

"All right," Vivian says, smoothing a stray hair back into her tidy bun. "I suppose we should get started."

NIAMH
NEW YORK CITY, 1929

Maisie sensed it first. She wouldn't stop crying.

Since Maisie was a month old she had slept with Niamh on her narrow cot. Their room was dark, with no windows; Niamh couldn't even see her brothers, Dominick and James, six-year-old twins, huddled together on their pallet on the floor.

She sat up on the cot with her back against the wall and held Maisie the way Mam had shown her, over her shoulder. She tried everything she could think of to comfort her, all the things that had worked before: stroking her back, running two fingers down the bridge of her little nose, humming their father's favorite song. "I have heard the blackbird pipe his note, the thrush and the linnet too / But there's none of them can sing so sweet, my singing bird, as you."

But Maisie only shrieked louder.

Only a few weeks after the baby was born, Mam had come down with a fever. She had no more milk for Maisie, so they made do with warm sweetened water, slow-cooked crushed oats, a splash of cow's milk when they could afford it.

Everyone in Niamh's family was thin; days went by when they had little more than rubbery potatoes in weak broth for supper. Eighteen-month-old Maisie weighed no more than a bundle of rags in Niamh's arms.

When Maisie finally stopped sobbing, Niamh held her close and the two of them drifted to sleep.

Mam screamed, and Niamh bolted awake, coughing from the acrid snoke in her nose. Then all was utter confusion.

Mam snatched Maisie from Niamh's arms and pushed her out into the hall. Da tried to wake James and Dominick, still asleep on the floor of their room. Probably the smoke had stupefied the boys, neighbors said later. Probably Da hadn't been able to rouse them. And then had not been able to get out himself.

Niamh found herself outside in the fresh, cold air. But Mam, holding Maisie, was not behind her. Maybe she'd turned back to look for Da. Maybe she'd missed her footing and stumbled.

If only Niamh had paid closer attention to why the baby was crying. If only she had realized that more was wrong than the hunger in Maisie's belly and the sweltering heat of the summer night. Maybe Maisie smelled smoke from the fire before any of the older children. Maybe she sensed, somehow, that danger was coming. If Niamh had listened and tried to understand, she might have been able to save her family.

Da, James, and Dominick had been carried out under white sheets. But men had carried Mam away on a stretcher, and Maisie was with her. There was still hope for them.

That was what Niamh clung to as she lay wrapped in a blanket on the floor of an unfamiliar room. She could hear Mr. and Mrs. Schatzman arguing.

"I didn't ask for this," Mrs. Schatzman hissed. "Those Irish! Too many children in too small a space. The only surprise is that this sort of thing doesn't happen more often."

This sort of thing, Niamh thought. This sort of thing meant half her family gone.

Somehow she fell asleep, her throat sore from tears and the harsh smoke. In the morning Mr. Schatzman woke her to tell her that he and Mrs. Schatzman had figured out a perfect solution. They would take her to the Children's Aid Society the next day. There were people there who helped children, he told Niamh. She'd be fed and warm and dry.

"I can't go," Niamh said. "My mother will need me when she gets out of the hospital."

He shook his head. "I'm sorry, child. She won't be coming back."

"But Maisie, then—" Niamh began.

"The doctors say that Margaret—that your sister—best not to hope," he told her awkwardly. He turned away, as if he didn't want to look at her, didn't want to see that his words had turned her entire life inside out.

Chapter Three

MOLLY
SPRUCE HARBOR, MAINE, PRESENT DAY

Bending down, Molly scans the labels on the cardboard boxes surrounding her. "Okay, so . . . I guess we start with the earliest first? This one says 'World War II.' Is there anything before that?"

"Yes." Vivian gets to her feet, squeezes between two stacks of boxes, and makes her way toward the cedar chests. She stops near a pile that looks ready to topple at her touch. "The earliest stuff is over here, I think."

Molly lifts the top box down to the floor. Scrawled on the top in faded marker are two dates: *1929–1930.* She takes her knife and pokes through the tape holding the box shut.

Vivian, sitting on a chest, waits patiently as Molly lifts out a mustard-colored coat.

"Mercy sake," she says. "I can't believe I saved that coat. I always hated it."

Molly holds the coat up, inspecting it. It's sort of a

military style with black buttons. The gray silk lining is coming to pieces, and something falls through a disintegrating pocket to bounce on the floor. A penny, dark with age.

Vivian gasps. Her face is pale. Molly looks closely at her, afraid she might have a heart attack or a stroke or something. Doesn't that happen to old people sometimes? But Vivian just says, a little sharply, "Could you find that, please?"

Molly lays the coat across a box and gets to her hands and knees. She fishes the coin out from under a cedar chest. She hasn't seen a penny like this before—on the front is Abraham Lincoln's familiar head, but on the back are two ears of wheat with the words ONE CENT in big letters in the middle. *Maybe that's how you get to be rich*, Molly thinks, *by making sure you keep track of every penny.*

Vivian holds out a hand and Molly drops the coin into it. "Is there anything else in the pockets?" Vivian asks. She still looks a little ashen. Molly wonders if she should call Terry, but it's not like Vivian has fallen over or can't talk or anything. If she wanted Terry, she could call for her herself.

Going through the coat's pockets, Molly discovers a folded piece of lined paper, worn almost to nothing at the creases. She unfolds it cautiously to find a child's careful script in faint pencil: *Upright and do right make all right. Upright and do right make all right. Upright and do right . . .*

Vivian takes the paper from her and spreads it out on her knee, looking more like herself now. "I remember doing this. I was copying Miss Larsen's writing on the board. She had the most beautiful penmanship."

"Your teacher?"

Vivian nods. "They barely teach handwriting anymore, I hear."

"Yeah, everything's on computer." Molly is suddenly struck by the fact that Vivian wrote these words on this sheet of paper at least eighty years ago, when she was a kid herself. Her mind boggles at the thought. Surely Vivian, a rich white lady in a big old house, was never anything like Molly. "Things have changed a lot since you were my age, huh?" she asks.

Vivian cocks her head, still studying the faded handwriting. "I suppose. Though not everything. I still sleep in a bed. Sit in a chair. Wash dishes in a sink."

Well, Terry washes dishes in a sink, Molly thinks.

"I don't watch much television. I don't need a computer. In a lot of ways my life is the same as it was twenty or even forty years ago."

"That's kind of sad," Molly blurts. And immediately regrets it.

23

But Vivian doesn't seem offended. "Do you think so? I don't think I've missed much."

"Well . . . only the internet, Snapchat, Facebook, smartphones, Instagram, YouTube . . ." Molly counts off on her fingers.

Vivian laughs. "I hardly think FaceTube—whatever that is—would improve my quality of life."

Molly shakes her head. "It's Face*book*. And You-Tube."

Vivian shrugs. "It doesn't make any difference to me."

Molly gives up. "Why did you keep this coat, if you hated it?" she asks.

Vivian picks up the coat gingerly and holds it out in front of her. "That's a very good question. But I have a question for you. Where is that mother of yours?"

Where did *that* question come from? "I don't know."

"Would you like to know?"

"No. I really don't care," Molly says shortly.

"You're not curious at all?"

"Nope."

"I'm not sure I believe that."

"Well, you should." Molly turns away from Vivian.

"Hmm. Because, actually, you seem kind of . . . angry."

"I'm not angry. I just don't want to talk about it,"

Molly says, making sure her voice says *that's enough.*
Even her social worker backs off when Molly uses that
voice. "So we should get rid of the coat, then? Put it on
the Goodwill pile? Or throw it out?"

Vivian folds the coat on her lap. "Ah . . . maybe. Let's
see what else is in this box."

NIAMH
NEW YORK CITY, 1929

"You—the Irish girl. Over here."

A thin, scowling matron in a white bonnet beckoned
with a bony finger. She must have known Niamh was
Irish from the papers Mr. Schatzman filled out when
he brought her in to the Children's Aid Society several weeks ago. Or maybe she could tell from Niamh's
accent, still as thick as peat.

There was a line of children behind Niamh on the
windy, chilly train platform. They'd been shuffling
forward for what seemed like forever, so that each child
could be inspected and checked off on a list. Finally it
was Niamh's turn.

She took a few steps forward to stand in front of the
skinny matron and a plump woman with a list in her
hand.

"Humph," the matron said, pursing her lips. "Red hair."

"Unfortunate," the plump woman agreed. "And those freckles! It's hard enough to get placed out at her age." She frowned at her paper. "Nee-AM? That's your name?"

"It's 'Neeve,'" Niamh said. A common enough name in County Galway, but Americans were always baffled by it.

The woman tsked and shook her head. "I hope you're not attached to that name, young miss," she said. "Because I can promise if you're lucky enough to be chosen, your new parents will change it in a second."

The thin matron licked her thumb and pushed the hair out of Niamh's face. "Don't want to scare them away, do you? You must keep it neat and pulled back." She pointed at Niamh's necklace. "What is that?"

Niamh reached up and touched the small pewter cross on a chain around her neck. At the center of the cross, where the arms met, two hands held a heart between them.

"It's an Irish cross. A Claddagh," she said, fighting the urge to clamp her fist around it.

"It's very odd-looking. What are those hands? And why does the heart have a crown?"

Niamh remembered what her gram said when she

gave her the cross. "The hands are for friendship. Holding hands, see? The heart is love. And the crown is loyalty."

The matron shook her head. "You're not allowed to bring keepsakes on the train."

Niamh's heart was pounding so hard she thought both women must be able to hear it. "It was my gran's."

The women peered at the cross. Niamh could see them hesitating, trying to decide what to do.

"She gave it to me in Ireland, before we came over. It's—it's the only thing I have left." This was true, and it was also true that she said it hoping the women would feel sorry for her and let her keep the necklace.

"All right, then," the plump one said finally, and called for the next child in line. Niamh joined the others waiting in a clump near the edge of the train platform.

There were about twenty of them, all ages, the girls in dresses with white pinafores and thick stockings, the boys in knickers that buttoned below the knee, white shirts, neckties, thick wool jackets. A tall woman in a black bonnet and a droopy, thin man with a droopy brown mustache guarded the group. Niamh remembered meeting them back at the Children's Aid: the man was Mr. Curran, and the woman was Mrs. Scatcherd. They'd be chaperones for the children on the train.

It was warm for October, and Niamh's braids stuck

to her neck. In one hand she clutched a small brown suitcase that held everything she owned in the world—a bible, two sets of clothes, a hat, a black coat several sizes too small, a pair of shoes. When she was admitted to the Children's Aid orphanage some weeks later, they gave her the clothes and this coat. Embroidered inside the coat was her name—Niamh Power.

Niamh heard the train before she could see it. A low hum, a rumble underfoot, a deep-throated whistle, faint at first and then louder as the train got close. Along with the other children, she craned her neck to look down the track, and suddenly, there it was: a black engine letting out a hiss of steam like a massive panting animal.

"Chil-dren! Places, children!" Mrs. Scatcherd shouted. They all lined up. Niamh felt lonelier than she ever had in her life. She'd lost her entire family. But her story, she knew, wasn't worse than the others. Every one of the children had a sad tale behind them—otherwise, they would not be there, about to step on a train and be carried away from the Children's Aid Society and New York City into a life they could not even begin to imagine.

Chapter Four

MOLLY
SPRUCE HARBOR, MAINE, PRESENT DAY

Molly is sitting with her social worker at a table in the school's science lab. All the other kids are eating lunch in the cafeteria. But Molly—lucky her—gets to eat with Lori every Tuesday.

"So how's the community service going?" Lori asks. She has bright eyes like shiny buttons and a small, pointy nose that, as far as Molly's concerned, she likes to stick in Molly's business.

Molly shrugs. She unwraps the sandwich Dina packed for her, a slice of baloney between two pieces of limp white bread.

Lori picks at the salad she packed in a Tupperware container. "I'll take that as an okay. But, Molly, you've really got to make an effort there. No more . . . problems, okay? We want things to go smoothly for you for a while."

It's not like Molly goes looking for problems. She'd love for everything to go smoothly for a while. It just never seems to work out that way. She peels apart the sandwich, pulls the baloney out of the middle, and leans over to drop it in a garbage can next to the table.

"You don't like baloney?" Lori asks.

"I'm a vegetarian," Molly says.

"Really? When did you decide that?"

"A few weeks ago." She'd been thinking about it for a while, but an online video about chicken farms convinced her.

"Have you told Mrs. Thibodeau?"

"Yeah." Molly puts the pieces of bread back together, picks up her sandwich of nothing, and takes a bite. Of course she told Dina. It hasn't stopped her from packing Molly a baloney sandwich every day.

"Hmm." Lori flips open a folder on her desk. "How are your classes going?"

Molly shrugs again.

Lori taps a pencil on a sheet of paper inside the folder. "There's a note from your Language Arts teacher."

"What'd she say?"

"She said she'd love for you to participate more in class. You haven't raised your hand once. Maybe you could give that a try. What do you think?"

Molly mushes the rest of the soft white bread into a ball and stuffs it into her mouth so she doesn't have to answer.

The truth is, she doesn't see the point of participating in class. Except for Jack, nobody really cares what she has to say anyway. She's just the weird Goth girl—even to her foster mother.

Molly touches her necklace, with its three charms: a blue-and-green fish, a pewter raven, and a tiny brown bear. She remembers the night her dad gave them to her and wishes that, right now, the charms would give her some kind of encouragement, some feeling of strength. *You can get through this.* Or maybe a warning. *Leave the science lab and run for it!*

But the charms feel like nothing. She can't even sense their weight against her skin.

Lori waits to see if Molly is going to say anything. Then she sighs and flips her folder shut. "Just stay out of trouble, Molly. Okay?"

Molly pulls a Red Delicious apple out of her lunch bag. It's a little soft to the touch and smells too sweet, like apples do when they're about to go bad. She takes a big bite, waiting for this time with Lori to be done.

NIAMH
NEW YORK CITY, 1929

Mrs. Scatcherd and Mr. Curran walked up and down the line, making sure that the children were all lined up by height, shortest to tallest. The babies were handed to girls older than eight. Mrs. Scatcherd pushed a toddler into Niamh's arms, an olive-skinned, slightly cross-eyed boy who seemed to be a few months younger than Maisie. "His name is Carmine, and he will be your charge," she said.

Brown suitcase in one hand, Carmine in the other, Niamh climbed unsteadily onto the high step that led into the train, wobbling until Mr. Curran scurried over to take the bag.

"Use some common sense, girl," he scolded. "If you fall, you'll crack both of your skulls, and then we'll have to leave the two of you behind."

Niamh found a seat inside the train, a bench long enough for her and Carmine to spread out, and Mr. Curran heaved her suitcase up on the rack over her head. Mrs. Scatcherd stood at the front of the car, holding on to the leather backs of two seats, the arms of her black cape draping like the wings of a crow.

"They call this an orphan train, children," she said in a shrill voice. "And you are lucky to be on it. You are leaving behind the big city, an evil place full of ignorance, poverty, and vice. You are on your way to a healthy and virtuous life in the country."

Niamh had lived in both the city and the country, and it never struck her that one was more honorable than the other. She bounced Carmine up and down on her lap.

"While you are on this train, you will follow some simple rules," Mrs. Scatcherd went on. "You will listen to instructions. You will not wander off alone at any time. And if your behavior proves to be a problem, you will be sent straight back to where you came from and left to fend for yourselves."

Niamh looked around at the faces of her fellow train riders. She knew some of the children from the time she'd spent at the Children's Aid Society. Others were strangers.

The younger ones, she saw, were wide-eyed and anxious and a little bewildered, as if worried that they might commit some dreadful sin without meaning to. The older ones looked like they were barely listening. Many of them had been at the Children's Aid for much longer than Niamh. Some had come there from other orphanages. They'd probably heard plenty of speeches like this before.

Carmine started to whine, kicking his feet against

Niamh's leg. He was hungry, she guessed. They'd only had a dry piece of bread and a tiny cup of milk for breakfast, and that was hours ago. But Niamh knew better than to ask when food would be coming. During her time in the orphanage, she'd learned that food came when adults were ready to pass it out, and not before.

At breakfast that morning she'd managed to drop two sugar lumps into her pocket. Now she crushed one between her fingers and licked her index finger to make the grains stick. She slipped the finger into Carmine's mouth. The look of astonished delight on his face made her smile.

After sucking her finger, Carmine seemed to relax. He clutched Niamh's hand with both of his chubby ones, holding on tight, and drifted off to sleep as the train started to move. Soon enough Niamh slept too.

She woke when they stopped at a depot. Through sleepy eyes she watched Mr. Curran get off. She could see him outside her window talking to the farmers on the platform. One held a basket of apples, one a sack full of bread. A man in a black apron reached into a box and unwrapped a package of brown paper to reveal a thick yellow slab of cheese, and Niamh's stomach rumbled.

Mr. Curran got back on the train, and it pulled out of the station. After a few minutes, Niamh saw a paper airplane winging above his head. Mr. Curran leaped to his feet and wheeled around. "Who did that?" he demanded, but no one confessed. Slowly he sat down. Then, from behind his back, someone let out a deafening belch.

Mr. Curran junped up again. "Scoundrels!"

More belches came from various benches, and one girl gave a high-pitched ghostly moan. Giggles burst out as Mr. Curran looked around wildly. Niamh put her face in Carmine's hair to hide her smile.

Mr. Curran could not pick out one child to punish. "I'll send you all off this train at the next stop!" he bellowed, standing in the aisle, gripping two seat backs for balance.

"I'd be glad to make my way on my own!" one of the older boys shot back. He had bold blue eyes under a flannel cap that was also blue, and he met Mr. Curran's gaze with defiance. "Been doing it for years. I reckon I can shine shoes in any city in America! It's probably better than being sent to live in a barn with animals, eating pig slops."

Children murmured in their seats.

"I hear we'll be sold at auction to the highest bidder," another boy whispered loudly.

The car grew silent. Mrs. Scatcherd, who had been silently watching all the commotion, stood up. In her black cloak and steel-rimmed glasses, she was far more frightening than Mr. Curran.

"I have heard enough," she snapped. "Mr. Curran, maybe the young man who spoke to you so impudently should be moved to a new seat." She lifted her chin, peering out from her bonnet like a turtle from its shell. "Ah—there's a space over there," she said, pointing a finger in Niamh's direction.

Niamh's skin prickled. But she could see that Mrs. Scatcherd meant what she said, so she slid as close as she could to the window. She set Carmine in the middle, a barrier between herself and this stranger.

The boy stood, pulled his bright blue cap down hard on his head, and dragged his feet up the aisle. He flung himself into the seat beside Carmine, then took his cap back off and slapped it against the seat in front. A small cloud of dust floated up.

"Man," he muttered, "what an old goat."

Then he held his finger out to Carmine, who buried his head in Niamh's lap.

"Don't get you nowhere being shy," the boy said. Glancing at Niamh, he said, "A redhead. That's worse than a bootblack. Who's gonna want you?"

Niamh's heart dropped. Hadn't those women on the train platform said the same thing? But she lifted her chin. "At least I'm not a criminal."

He laughed. "That's what I am, am I?"

"You tell me."

"Would you believe me?"

"Probably not."

"No point, then, is there."

Niamh didn't answer, and they sat in silence. Outside the window, gray clouds hung low in a watery sky.

"They took my kit from me," the boy said after a while.

Niamh turned to look at him. "What?"

"My bootblack kit. All my paste and brushes. How do they expect me to make a living?"

"They don't. They're going to find you a family."

"You think so, huh?" he said. "A ma to tuck us in at night and a pa to put food on the table? I don't see it working out like that. Do you?"

"I don't know. Haven't thought about it," she said, though it was all she could think about.

"Well, I have," he said. Over the next few hours the boy told Niamh his story. His name was Hans, but everybody called him Dutchy. His mother died of pneumonia, and his father sent him out into the streets to earn money as a bootblack, beating him with a belt if he didn't bring back enough. So one day he stopped going home.

He fell in with a gang of boys on the streets, and they looked after one another as much as they could.

He taught himself piano by ear in the back room of a speakeasy, where people crept in to order beer and whiskey they couldn't buy in the light of day, not since the law changed. And then someone from the Children's Aid Society came by and promised him a hot meal if he came inside—and he ended up here, sitting beside Niamh on this train full of orphans.

When Carmine began to fuss, Dutchy reached into his pocket and pulled out a penny. He rolled it across his fingers, held it between his thumb and forefinger, touched it to Carmine's nose, and then clasped it in his closed fist. When he opened his hand, the penny wasn't there. He reached behind Carmine's ear, and—"Presto," Dutchy said.

Carmine gazed at the bright coin between Dutchy's fingers, astonished.

Dutchy grinned at Niamh and tucked the coin back into his pocket. "Who knows what'll happen to us? If it's bad we just have to put up with it. Or maybe we'll get lucky and live happily ever after. Only the good Lord knows what's next, and he ain't telling."

Chapter Five

MOLLY
SPRUCE HARBOR, MAINE, PRESENT DAY

Molly is sitting at the desk in her room, doing math. The only thing on the surface of her desk is her textbook and a sheet of lined paper.

She opens her desk drawer and reaches in to find a pencil sharpener, neatly set alongside a packet of yellow Post-its, a row of unsharpened pencils, three ballpoint pens, and a stapler. She gives her pencil a perfect point.

Jack, who's sitting on the floor by Molly's bed with a textbook open on his knees, snorts. Molly looks over at him. "What?"

"That's the third time you've sharpened your pencil since you started your homework."

"So?" Molly glowers at him. She likes her pencils sharp. What's wrong with that? Her numbers look neater that way.

Jack puts up a hand as if to shield himself from her glare.

Dina passes by in the hall and looks in suspiciously. "Only if the door is wide open," she said when Molly asked if Jack could come over and study with her after school.

"He's not my boyfriend!" Molly said. "Just a friend."

"Wide. Open," Dina said. "Or he's not coming."

"Okay, okay."

When Molly told Jack what Dina had said, he shrugged. "I get it. Moms can be annoying."

"She's not my mom," Molly snapped.

Jack just laughed. "I think you both need to chill out a little bit."

Molly met Jack her first week here, in Language Arts. They'd been assigned to a writing group, along with Jody Davis. Jody tucked a strand of long, taffy-colored hair behind her ear and stared at Molly. "That girl is weird," Molly heard her whisper to Jack. "She freaks me out."

Jack didn't do what Molly expected. He didn't laugh at Molly or exchange an *I know, right?* look with Jody. He just shrugged. Then, when Jody looked away, he glanced at Molly, ran a finger down his own hair where the blue streak was in hers, and grinned.

Molly tugs at the blue streak, remembering. In between math problems, she's been sketching a shape on the edge of her paper. A circle the size of a quarter, with four legs, a head, and a tail. Now she begins to draw in a tiny, tight pattern on the turtle's shell.

"Hey, what's that?"

Molly looks up, startled. She'd become so interested in her drawing that she hadn't noticed Jack closing his book or coming to stand over her. Instinctively she covers the turtle with her hand, but Jack's already seen it.

"Cool. What's his name?"

"It doesn't have a name."

"I think you should call him Carlos."

"What?" Despite herself, Molly begins to smile. She takes her hand away and studies the turtle. "Why Carlos?"

"He just looks like a Carlos. See his little head? He's kind of wagging it, like, 'What's up?' He's a chill dude." Jack perches on the edge of her desk. "So . . . how's it going with Mrs. Daly?"

"Vivian." Molly folds the sheet of math problems in half and puts it away in her textbook, turtle and all. "Oh, I don't know. She's all up in my business."

"Like how?"

"I don't know anything about her life. Oh, except she said that one of her teachers when she was in school was named Miss Larsen. Not like I care! But she expects me to tell her everything about mine! What does she need to know for?"

"Maybe she's lonely. Living in that big house all by herself. My mom is the only one she talks to."

Molly frowns. "Well, I don't need to tell her stories about my sad life. We can't all be rich and live in mansions."

"So turn it around. Ask her questions."

"Like what?"

"Like whatever," Jack says. "You're going through all those boxes, right? So ask some questions about what she's kept up there all these years. Like: Why turtles?"

Molly looks at him as if he's lost his mind.

He nods at her notebook. "'Why turtles?' See, that's how you ask people questions. You like them?"

"Are you asking me?"

He nods.

"Turtles—they mean something. In my culture."

"Like what?"

Why should she answer him? Or Vivian? Or Lori? Dina walks by the room for a second time and stares at him, and he ignores her. He's just sitting there looking at Molly, smiling a little. He actually seems to want to know about the turtles.

Molly opens her notebook again and looks at Carlos. "Turtles carry their homes on their backs," she tells

42

Jack, remembering what her dad told her years ago. She repeats his words as best she can. "They're out there in the world, for anyone to see, but hidden at the same time. They're strong. They're slow, but they get where they're going. They don't give up."

She draws another turtle next to Carlos, a little smaller, with a different pattern on its shell. Jack sits next to her quietly, watching her pencil on the paper.

It's funny. Sitting at her desk with Jack, with Dina pacing back and forth in the hall outside like she's on patrol, Molly feels exposed and protected all at once. Yeah, that's right. Like a turtle in a shell.

NIAMH
CHICAGO, ILLINOIS, 1929

On the third day the train crossed the Illinois state line. Niamh felt stiff and sore from all the hours on the hard bench, restless and tired at once, and amazed by the sheer size of the United States. She'd known the country was big, but she had no idea how big. They had been traveling for days and were barely in the middle yet!

Near Chicago, Mrs. Scatcherd stood for another lecture. "In a few minutes we will arrive at Union Station, where we'll switch trains for the next portion of our journey," she told the children. "We are not allowed to board for an hour, so we will wait on the platform. Quietly. Young men, put on your suit coats. Young ladies, your pinafores.

"Chicago is a proud and noble city, on the edge of a great lake. The lake makes it windy, which is why it is called the Windy City. You will bring your suitcases, of course, and will want to put on your coats. Mr. Curran and I expect you to conduct yourselves like the model citizens the Children's Aid Society believes you can become."

Mrs. Scatcherd was right; when Niamh stepped off the train, the wind on the platform rushed through her pinafore and her dress. She dug her too-small coat out of her suitcase and stuffed her arms into the sleeves, but it was impossible to fasten the buttons. Carmine staggered around, happy to have room to roam, while Niamh kept a sharp eye on him. He wanted to know the name of everything he saw: Train. Wheel. Lights.

They were a quiet lot, even the older boys, who were huddled together, stamping their feet to keep warm.

Except for Dutchy, Niamh realized. Where did he go?

"Psst. Niamh."

When she heard her name, she turned to glimpse his blond head at the foot of a staircase across the platform.

Niamh looked over at the adults. Mrs. Scatcherd was

frowning at a conductor. Mr. Curran was poring over papers with a station agent. A large rat scurried along a brick wall a little way down the platform. As the other children pointed and shrieked, Niamh scooped Carmine up and slipped behind a pillar and a pile of wooden crates.

In the stairwell, Dutchy leaned against a wall. When he saw Niamh, he turned and bounded up the stairs, vanishing around a corner. Niamh held Carmine tightly and followed.

She knew perfectly well that she shouldn't be doing this, and she told herself she only wanted to find Dutchy to make him come back—but for the first time since the dreadful night when she had lost her family, something flickered inside her. It wasn't quite happiness and it wasn't quite hope, but it might have been curiosity. What was at the top of the staircase? What did Chicago look like beyond this one platform?

Carmine tilted his head up and leaned back in her arms, floppy as a sack of rice. "Yite," he murmured, pointing. Following his gaze, she saw that just up ahead was the enormous ceiling of the train station, laced with skylights.

They stepped into the huge terminal, filled with people. There were wealthy women in furs, trailed by servants. Men in top hats and morning coats. Shopgirls in bright dresses. Dutchy was standing in the middle, looking up at the sky through the huge panes of glass, with a huge grin on his face. Suddenly he took off his cap and flung it into the air.

Carmine struggled in Niamh's arms, and when she set him down, he raced toward Dutchy and grabbed his legs. Dutchy reached down and hoisted the baby onto his shoulders. He clasped Carmine's legs and began to twirl.

Carmine stretched out his arms and threw back his head, shrieking with glee, and that flicker inside Niamh sharpened and brightened into joy. Joy so sharp it felt like the edge of a knife. Even though it hurt, she hugged the feeling tightly. It was nothing she'd ever experienced before, and she didn't know if she'd ever feel it again.

A whistle blasted through the air. Niamh spun around, trying to see where the sound had come from. She spotted three policemen in dark uniforms, racing toward Dutchy and Carmine. Mrs. Scatcherd had climbed the stairs from the platform. She raised her black wing, pointing toward the two boys. Mr. Curran pushed past her. Dutchy froze. Carmine grabbed his hair and shrieked.

Just then someone seized hold of Niamh's arm, another policeman. "Trying to get away, were you?" he hissed in her ear, his breath smelling of licorice.

Niamh twisted in his grasp, trying to see what had happened to Dutchy. He was facedown on the ground now, the policemen surrounding him. Carmine was on the ground as well, sitting beside Dutchy, crying and bewildered. Niamh tried to go to him, but the policeman yanked her back. Then another policeman hauled Dutchy roughly to his feet, and they were both dragged over to Mrs. Scatcherd. A third policeman carried Carmine.

"These are your charges, ma'am?" one of the policemen asked.

Mrs. Scatcherd nodded. "Unfortunately they are." She looked as if she'd bitten into a lime. "I placed this young man with you," she said to Niamh in a quietly terrible voice, "in the hope that you might prove a civilizing influence. It appears that I was gravely mistaken."

Niamh wanted to tell her that Dutchy didn't mean any harm, that she didn't either, that both of them just wanted to see what was at the top of the stairwell, that they just wanted to spin and laugh under the bright sky. "No, ma'am, I—"

"Do not interrupt."

Niamh looked down.

"Now, what do you have to say for yourself?"

"I'm sorry."

Niamh knew that Mrs. Scatcherd was not going to approve of her, never again. But maybe she could still save Dutchy. If Mrs. Scatcherd sent him off the train here, in Chicago, what would he do? He didn't have his bootblack kit. He couldn't make money for himself.

"I asked Dutchy—I mean Hans—to take me and the baby into the station," she told Mrs. Scatcherd. "I thought . . . maybe we could get a glimpse of that lake. I thought the baby would like to see it."

Mrs. Scatcherd glared at her. Dutchy looked startled but said nothing. Carmine said, "Yake?"

Mrs. Scatcherd's face softened.

"You are a foolish and headstrong girl," she told Niamh, but her voice had lost its edge, and Niamh could tell that she wasn't as angry as she wanted to appear. "You disobeyed my instructions. You've disgraced yourself." She turned to the officers in their uniforms. "But this is not, I think, a matter for the police."

The officer holding Dutchy let him go.

MOLLY
SPRUCE HARBOR, MAINE, PRESENT DAY

After Jack has packed up his backpack and gone home, Dina calls from the kitchen that dinner is ready.

"So how's that community service working out?" Ralph asks when Molly gets to the table. He pours himself a big glass of milk.

"Fine," Molly says. She picks up a piece of corn on the cob from a platter in the center of the table and plucks a hot dog gingerly from the bun on her plate. She sets the meat quietly to one side. "There's lots of stuff in that attic."

"Twenty hours' worth?" asks Dina.

"I guess there's other things I can do if we finish the attic," Molly says. "That house is huge."

"Yeah, sure is. I know the house—I've done some plumbing work over there," Ralph says. "Old pipes. Is Jack's mom usually there when you're working?"

Molly nods. "She's around. Doing laundry and stuff."

Dina gives her a funny smile. "Terry Gallant doing laundry. Now there's a picture."

Molly looks at her in confusion.

"Come on, Dina," Ralph says mildly.

Dina ignores him. "Back in high school, Terry Gallant was Miss Popular. Homecoming queen and all that," she tells Molly. "Now she's scrubbing floors, huh?"

Molly turns her attention to her food. When she's done, she picks up her plate with the hot dog still on it. She remembers to thank Dina for dinner.

By the time they left Chicago, it was evening. As the train chugged out of the station, Mrs. Scatcherd rapped Dutchy's knuckles several times with a long wooden ruler as punishment for leaving the platform. He barely winced, then shook his hands twice in the air and winked at Niamh.

Carmine sat on Niamh's lap, face pressed against the window, gazing out at the streets and buildings, all lit up. "Yite," he said softly as Dutchy flopped onto the seat beside him.

"Get a good night's rest, children," Mrs. Scatcherd called from the front of the car. "In the morning we'll be making our first stop. You will need to be at your very best if you want to be chosen by a kind family."

"What if nobody wants me?" one boy asked, and the entire car seemed to hold its breath.

Mrs. Scatcherd looked as if she'd been waiting for this. "If it happens that you are not chosen at the first stop, there will be several later chances. I cannot think of a time . . ." She paused. "It is very rare for a child to be with us on the return trip to New York."

"Pardon me, ma'am," a girl near the front said. "What if I don't want to go with the people who choose me?"

"What if they're mean?" a younger boy cried out.

"Children!" Mrs. Scatcherd's glasses flashed as she turned her head from side to side. "I will not have you interrupting!"

But was she going to answer the questions or not? Everybody had their eyes on her.

"I will say this." She looked sterner than ever. "Some parents are looking for a healthy boy to work on the farm. Some people want babies. Parents sometimes think they want one thing, but later change their minds. We dearly hope all of you will find the right home at the first stop, but it doesn't always work out that way. Be respectable, polite, and keep your faith in God. Whether your journey is long or short, He will help you as long as you place your trust in Him."

Niamh looked at Dutchy. Mrs. Scatcherd hadn't really answered the question—but the message was clear. Mrs. Scatcherd did not know, any more than the children knew, whether they'd be treated with kindness. This train was taking them steadily into the unknown, and they had no choice but to sit quietly in their hard seats and let themselves be taken there.

Chapter Six

MOLLY
SPRUCE HARBOR, MAINE, PRESENT DAY

Molly is starting to figure out that "cleaning out the attic" actually means taking things out of boxes, looking at them for a few minutes, and putting them back where they were.

After a week of going through Vivian's stuff, the pile of things to throw out or give away is tiny. A short stack of musty books. A few sheets and pillowcases, yellow with time.

"I don't think I'm helping you much," she tells Vivian one afternoon in the attic.

"Well, maybe not," says Vivian. "But I'm helping you, aren't I?"

Molly twitches inside and clamps her mouth shut. Does that mean Vivian knows about the stolen book? That Molly has to do her hours to stay at Ralph and Dina's?

"With your service project," Vivian adds, looking

at Molly a little strangely, as if she's wondering why Molly seems panicked.

Molly sticks her head into a cedar chest and pulls out an old-fashioned brown dress with pearl buttons down the front, the kind of thing, Molly thinks, that you might see on an American Girl doll. Not that Molly ever had one, but she's seen the catalogs. Next to the dress is a crumpled turquoise cardigan, embroidered flowers fraying, green leaves springing loose from their stitches.

Under the sweater Molly uncovers a green hardcover book with the words *Anne of Green Gables* stamped on the front in gold.

"Hand me that," Vivian says. She takes it and opens it to an illustration of a wide-eyed girl with her red hair in two braids. "Ah, yes, I remember," she says. "I was not much older than you when I read this for the first time. A teacher gave it to me—you remember. Miss Larsen. 'Upright and do right make all right.'"

Molly does remember that it was Miss Larsen who'd made Vivian copy out that sentence. She can't imagine having a favorite teacher who'd assign a boring writing exercise like that, but Vivian is smiling. She leafs through the pages.

"Anne talks so much, doesn't she? I was much shyer than that." She looks up. "What about you?"

"Sorry, I haven't read it," Molly says. She wishes Vivian would stop talking about books. Is she hinting that she knows? Does she want Molly to confess?

Well, if Vivian wants her to say something, she can just ask. Until then, Molly is keeping her mouth shut. She pulls more things out of the chest—clothes, book, knickknacks wrapped in old newspaper—and sets them on the floor.

"No, no, I mean, were you shy as a girl? What am I saying—you still are a girl. But I mean when you were younger?"

"Not exactly shy. I was—quiet." *Still am*, she thinks.

"Circumspect," Vivian says.

Molly looks at her a little suspiciously. "What does that mean?"

"Watchful," says Vivian. "Careful. Reserved."

That seems about right. Molly is surprised—how does this old lady know her so well? Teachers always complain that Molly is sullen, that she won't speak up in class, that she doesn't try to make friends. That's what Lori was getting at, the last time they had lunch. Nobody seems to realize that she's watching and waiting, trying to decide if it's safe to speak up.

Vivian closes the book. "You strike me as a reader. Am I right?"

Molly shrugs. This feels like a trap. At any moment,

Vivian is going to spring it on her.

"So what's your favorite book?"

"I don't know. I don't have one."

"Oh, I think you probably do. You're the type."

Molly jerks upright. "What's that supposed to mean?" The type to steal a book? The type to lie about it to an old lady who needs help with her attic?

But Vivian's face is not accusing—merely interested. "I can tell that you feel things. Deeply." She leans forward and, to Molly's surprise, presses the book into her hands. "No doubt you'll find this old-fashioned. Sentimental, even. But I want you to have it."

"You're giving it to me?"

"Why not?"

Molly looks down at the book. She nearly got thrown out of her foster home for stealing a book. She's only here in this attic because she stole a book. And now Vivian just hands her one. As if it's that easy!

"Do I have to read it?" she mutters.

"Absolutely. There will be a quiz," Vivian says with a twinkle in her eye.

Despite herself, Molly smiles. "I'm terrible at quizzes."

"I doubt that very much," Vivian says. "Anyway—I hope you'll like it."

"Well— Thank you." She holds the book to her

chest before setting it beside her on the floor. Then she picks up an ancient pair of brown mittens that look like they've been gnawed on by a mouse. Maybe several mice. "I can get rid of these, right?"

Vivian takes the bedraggled mittens from Molly's hand. "I think maybe I'll hang on to them," she says. Which is what she says just about every time Molly asks that question.

NIAMH
MILWAUKEE ROAD DEPOT, MINNEAPOLIS, MINNESOTA, 1929

Niamh slept badly on the train the night they reached Minnesota. At dawn she was wide awake, so full of nervous energy she could feel the blood pumping through her heart.

She untied the ribbon in her hair and let it fall to her shoulders. Then she combed through it with her fingernails and pulled it back, as tightly as she could. Turning, she caught Dutchy looking at her.

"Your hair is pretty," he said.

She squinted at him to see if he was teasing.

"That's not what you said a few days ago."

"I said redheads have a hard time getting chosen.

Not that I don't like it." He shrugged. "Can't help what you are, can you?"

Niamh craned her neck to see if Mrs. Scatcherd might've heard them talking, but there was no movement toward the front of the train car. Most of the other children were still asleep. Carmine snored a little, his head on Niamh's lap, his little feet on Dutchy's leg.

Dutchy wrapped a hand around Carmine's feet. "I never said thanks."

"For what?"

"For what you did at the train station. You could have told them it was all my idea, going up to the waiting room. You were just following me."

"I wouldn't have done that," Niamh said, a little indignantly.

"I know. But there's a lot who would." Dutchy leaned forward a little. "Listen. Wherever we go, let's try to find each other."

"How can we? We'll probably end up in different places."

"That's true."

"And my name will be changed."

"Mine too, maybe. But we can try."

Niamh hesitated. "Back at the orphanage they said we should make a clean slate. Let go of the past."

"I can let go of the past, no problem." Dutchy picked up a wool blanket that had fallen to the floor and tucked it around the lump of Carmine's body. "But I don't want to forget everything."

Niamh nodded. She felt that way too.

Outside the window, she could see three sets of tracks parallel to the one their train was on, and beyond them broad flat fields of furrowed soil. The sky was clear and blue. The train car smelled of diaper rags and sweat and sour milk.

Mrs. Scatcherd stood. "All right, children. Wake up!" She clapped her hands several times. Around her, Niamh heard small grunts and sighs as the children who were lucky enough to have fallen asleep opened their eyes and stretched their cramped arms and legs.

"Clean faces, combed hair, shirts tucked in," Mrs. Scatcherd said briskly. "Big ones, please assist the little ones. Bright eyes and smiles. You will not fidget or touch your faces. And you will say what, Rebecca?"

"Please and thank you," a girl with blond ringlets murmured sleepily.

"Please and thank you what?"

"Please and thank you, ma'am."

"You will wait to speak until you are spoken to. And then you will say please and thank you, ma'am. You will wait to do what? Andrew?"

"Speak until you are spoken to?" a brown-haired boy guessed.

"Exactly. The good citizens of Minneapolis are coming to the meeting hall today with the intention of taking one of you home—possibly more than one. So remember, girls, tie your hair ribbons neatly. Boys, button your shirts. Do everything in your power to make it easy for a new family to choose you. Is that clear?"

The train pulled into the station with a high-pitched squealing of brakes and a great gust of steam. Carmine was quiet, gaping at the buildings and wires and people outside the window.

Niamh wanted to say something to Dutchy, but she could not think what. Her hands were clammy. It was a terrible kind of anticipation, not knowing what they were walking into.

They lined up in the aisle, Niamh with the solid weight of Carmine in her arms, Dutchy carrying their bags.

"Quickly, children," Mrs. Scatcherd said. "In two straight lines. That's good." Her tone was gentler than usual. "This way." They followed her off the train and up a wide stone staircase. Mr. Curran brought up the rear.

At the top of the stairs they made their way down a corridor lit by glowing gas lamps and into the main waiting room of the station. It was not as big or as beautiful as the one in Chicago, but it was bright, with large windows.

People pointed and whispered. Niamh wondered if they knew why the children were here. And then she spotted a printed paper attached to a column. In black block letters, it read:

WANTED
Homes for Orphan Children
A Company of Homeless Children from the East
will arrive at
Milwaukee Road Depot, Friday, October 18.
Distribution will take place at 10 a.m.
These children are of various ages and both sexes,
having been thrown friendless upon the world . . .

As if someone had turned a crank in her back, Niamh shuffled forward, one foot after another. She smelled something sweet—candy apples?—as she passed a vendor's cart. How strange, she thought, that she'd ended up in a place her parents and brothers and sister had never been and never would be. How strange that she was here and they were gone.

She touched the Claddagh cross around her neck.

Ahead, Mrs. Scatcherd stood beside a large oak door.

When the children reached her, they gathered around in a semicircle, the older girls holding babies and the younger children holding hands. Niamh's stomach felt hollow and trembly.

Mrs. Scatcherd nodded. "All right, Mr. Curran. We are ready."

Mr. Curran leaned against the large door with his shoulder, pushing it open.

Chapter Seven

MOLLY
SPRUCE HARBOR, MAINE, PRESENT DAY

For the past week in Molly's social studies class they've been studying the Wabanaki Indians. For the first time since she started at Spruce Harbor Middle School, Molly's been sort of interested. Anyway, it's better than diagramming sentences in Language Arts, that's for sure.

Molly already knew that Wabanaki means "People of the Dawnland," because they lived where the first light of day touches the American continent. But Mr. Reed's been telling them some stuff she didn't know, like the fact that the Wabanaki are actually a confederacy of five tribes, including the Penobscot—Molly's own tribe—that live near the North Atlantic coast.

Last week, they went on a field trip to the Abbe, a museum about Native American culture in Bar Harbor. Molly lingered by the Penobscot baskets, made out of sweetgrass and bark from birch trees and brown ash.

This week, Mr. Reed is telling them about their final project. It'll be worth a third of their grade.

"Portaging," Mr. Reed says. "Everybody remember what portaging is?"

Molly remembers learning about portaging at the Abbe Museum, but she doesn't raise her hand. Mr. Reed focuses on her anyway. "Molly?"

Molly sighs, but speaks up. "Well. In the old days, the Wabanaki had to carry their canoes and everything they owned across land from one body of water to the next. When they came to the end of one lake or river or whatever, they had to pack up and bring it all on their backs."

Mr. Reed nods. "Thank you, Molly. So if you know you're going to have to portage, you think carefully about what to pack, right? You need to travel light. You take what's essential, what you can't live without, and you leave the rest behind."

Molly touches her necklace.

"For this project, I want you to interview someone in your family. Someone older. Your mother or father, a grandparent, someone who's lived through things you haven't. And ask them about a time they had to take a journey of some kind. Maybe it was an actual journey, maybe just a change of life, trying something new. Ask what they took with them from their old life and what they decided to leave behind. You'll turn the answers they give you into a report for the class."

Mr. Reed starts the kids off brainstorming questions they can ask during their interviews. "You can ask if they brought photo albums!" Megan McDonald calls out, two seats in front of Molly.

Other kids add suggestions. Mr. Reed scribbles them all on the board. "Get out your notebooks and write these down," he tells everybody.

Molly pulls out a notebook and begins to write, but she doesn't raise her hand to add anything. She's too busy wondering who she's going to talk to.

If her father were still alive, she'd pick him. Maybe she'd write about how he named his only daughter after Molly Molasses, a Penobscot Indian born the year before America declared its independence. She'd lived into her nineties—like Vivian, Molly thinks—coming and going from Indian Island, where Molly herself was born. The Penobscots said Molly Molasses had powers, *m'teoulin*, given by the Great Spirit. People with those powers, her dad told her, could interpret what dreams meant, cure diseases, and tell hunters where to find game.

It's too bad Molly didn't wind up with any of those powers herself. Maybe if she had, she wouldn't have been moved around so much from one place to another.

Maybe she would've been born to a mom capable of remembering that a kid needs to be fed now and then. Maybe she could even have protected her dad from that car accident.

But she didn't. And her dad's not here, so she can't write about any of that.

She could interview Ralph or Dina. But she cringes at the thought. It would be like she's *trying* to get them to be her mom and dad, or something. Ugh.

So how is Molly going to make this project work?

NIAMH
MILWAUKEE ROAD DEPOT, MINNEAPOLIS, MINNESOTA, 1929

Niamh stood at the back of the large, windowless, wood-paneled room, with Carmine in her arms and Dutchy right behind her. The room was filled with rows of people sitting in chairs, murmuring and looking back at the children. Mrs. Scatcherd motioned to the children to follow her down the center aisle. As she led them toward a low stage at the front, the crowd quieted row by row.

Surely, Niamh hoped, someone here would want her. Maybe she'd go to live in a bright, sunny house, where there would be warm cake to eat and tea with as much sugar as she wanted.

But she was quaking as she made her way up the stairs to the stage, hugging Carmine tight.

They lined up by height, smallest to tallest. Though Dutchy was three years older than Niamh, she was tall for her age, and they were only separated by one boy in the line.

Mr. Curran cleared his throat and began to make a speech. He asked the crowd to remember that they would be doing a good deed, saving a child from poverty and sin and depravity. He talked about the paperwork. He said that the families watching could have a child for free, but they would have to feed and clothe that child and send him or her to school. At first it would be a ninety-day trial. If they didn't like their choice after ninety days, they could send the child back.

The girl beside Niamh made a low noise like a dog's whine and slipped her hand into Niamh's.

The adults lined up and began to climb the stairs to the stage. Niamh felt like one of the cows for sale at the market in her village in Ireland.

In front of her, now, stood a young blond woman, slight and pale. An earnest young man was beside her, wearing a felt hat. The woman stepped forward. "May I?"

"Excuse me?" Niamh said.

The woman held out her arms. She wanted Carmine. He took one look and buried his face in Niamh's neck.

"He's shy." Niamh jiggled him, trying to get him to look up.

"Hello, little boy," the woman said. "What's your name?"

Carmine peeked up at her and nestled his warm, sticky cheek against Niamh's neck.

"The crossed eyes can be fixed, don't you think?" the woman said to her husband.

"I don't know. I would reckon so," he answered.

The woman stroked Carmine's arm with her finger. "Sweet thing," she murmured.

He picked his head up and gave her a bashful smile.

She looked at her husband. "I think he's the one."

"Nice lady," Niamh whispered to Carmine, swallowing a lump in her throat. "She wants to be your mam."

"Mam?" he said, his warm breath on her face.

"His name is Carmine," Niamh told the people. Reaching up, she pried the little boy's monkey arms from around her neck.

The woman put her hand on Carmine's back, and he squirmed away from her and clung to Niamh even more tightly. "No, no, no," he insisted.

"Do you need a girl to help with him?" Niamh

blurted out. "I could—" She thought wildly, trying to remember what she was good at. "I know about babies. I took care of my little sister. And I can mend clothes. And cook."

The woman's face filled with pity. "Oh, child," she said. "I am sorry. We can't afford two. We just—we came here for a baby. I'm sure you'll find . . ." Her voice trailed off.

Niamh pushed back tears. Carmine started to whimper. "You must go to your new mam," she told him firmly, and peeled him off her neck.

She would not cry, she told herself fiercely. She would stay polite and neat and she would smile and say please and thank you.

The woman took Carmine awkwardly. Niamh guessed that she was not used to holding a baby. She reached out and tucked the little boy's legs under his new mother's arm.

"Thank you for taking care of him," the woman said.

Before Niamh could answer, Mrs. Scatcherd swooped over and herded the young couple and Carmine off the stage. Niamh felt as if a piece of her heart had left with him.

One by one, the children around Niamh were chosen. The boy between Dutchy and Niamh went off with a short, round woman who told him it was high time she had a man around the house. The girl who'd held Niamh's hand went off with a stylish couple in hats. Dutchy and Niamh were standing, talking quietly, when a man came closer. His skin was as tan and scuffed as old shoe leather. A sour-looking woman trailed behind him.

The man eyed them for a minute without a word. Then he reached out and squeezed Dutchy's arm.

"What're you doing?" Dutchy asked, startled.

"Open your mouth."

Niamh could see Dutchy's hand closing into a fist. But Mr. Curran had come up behind them, so Dutchy didn't dare throw a punch. The man stuck a dirty-looking finger into Dutchy's mouth.

Dutchy jerked his head away.

"Ever work as a hay baler?" the man asked.

Dutchy stared straight ahead.

"You hear me, son?"

"No."

"No, you didn't hear me?"

Dutchy looked at him. "Never worked as a hay baler. I don't even know what that is."

"What do you think?" the man asked the woman. "He's a tough one, but we could use a kid this size."

"I reckon he'll fall into line," she said. "We break horses. Boys aren't that different."

It was just as Dutchy predicted, Niamh thought. Country people looking for free labor. They walked off with Mr. Curran without a glance at Dutchy.

"Maybe it won't be that bad," she whispered.

"If he lays a hand on me . . ." Dutchy glared at the farmer's retreating back.

"They have to send you to school."

He laughed. "And what'll happen to them if they don't? Who's even going to check?"

"You'll make them send you," Niamh insisted.

"Hey, boy! Stop your dallying," the man called, clapping his hands so loudly that everyone turned to look.

Dutchy reached into his pocket and slipped a penny into Niamh's hand, the one he'd used for his magic trick to make Carmine laugh. "For luck."

"You need it too."

"I know my fate, don't I? Looks like you're the one getting back on that train."

Then he walked across the stage and down the steps, waving at Niamh with a sad smile as he joined the couple who'd chosen him. Niamh was alone again.

Chapter Eight

MOLLY
SPRUCE HARBOR, MAINE, PRESENT DAY

Once she gets home from school, Molly takes the vacuum cleaner out of the closet in the hallway and runs it over the carpet in her room, careful to get into every corner. She pulls the quilt loose from her bed and tucks it in again, making sure the corners are sharp. There are a few pieces of crumpled-up paper and a Skittles wrapper in the little trash can by her desk, so she picks it up and carries it to the kitchen.

Dina is home from work early, and she's putting away dishes from the dishwasher. She snorts softly as Molly nudges past her to empty her trash into the big bin under the sink. "Why don't you clean up the living room if you've got so much energy?" she says, dumping silverware into a drawer.

Molly doesn't answer, retreating to her room as quickly as she can. She flops down on the perfectly made bed, staring up at the ceiling.

Straightening up usually makes her feel better. But today it doesn't. Molly knows perfectly well why her mood is as sour as month-old milk. It's that portaging project. It never seems to occur to teachers that not everybody has a big family at home—a mother, a father, grandparents, all eager to help out.

Mr. Reed's pretty nice, and if Molly tells him she doesn't have anyone to interview, he'll probably let her do something different. But Molly is sick of explaining to people why she's not the same as everybody else.

She pulls her phone out of her pocket and calls Jack. "What's up?" he asks.

"Do you have to do some kind of portaging project for social studies?" she asks.

"Some kind of what?"

"Portaging project. Portaging is—never mind. The thing is, I've got to interview somebody. Somebody old. Mr. Reed said maybe our grandparents, but obviously . . ."

She figures Jack will understand. His family isn't exactly like a Norman Rockwell painting either. His dad was a migrant worker, picking blueberries, when he met Jack's mom. Before Jack was even born, the guy made his way back to the Dominican Republic. Terry stayed in Spruce Harbor and raised Jack on her own.

"Yeah," Jack says. "I get it. I remember when we had

to do a family tree in fourth grade. I couldn't fill out any of the stuff for my dad's side. I turned in half a tree."

Molly laughs a little.

"But this project will be easy."

Molly frowns. "What do you mean?"

"See, you should listen to me more. Didn't I already tell you to ask Vivian questions?"

"Vivian?" Molly sits up with surprise.

"Why not?"

"Well, it's supposed to be a family member."

"Just check with your teacher," Jack says. "I'm sure it'll be okay."

He's probably right that Mr. Reed would agree to it. And Vivian is certainly the oldest person Molly's ever met.

For some reason, though, she feels like she has to argue with Jack. "But it's not like Vivian had a big, dramatic life or anything," she says. "She was adopted and grew up in Minnesota. Her parents had a department store. She ran it. Then she retired and moved to Maine. Her life sounds pretty boring."

"Who cares if it's boring?" Jack says. "You just need a passing grade."

"Maybe she won't talk to me."

"Maybe you should just ask, huh?"

Jack's right. Molly knows he's right.

"Okay, I'll ask," she mumbles. "I bet she'll say no, though."

"Portage?" Vivian looks quizzical. "That sounds like— oh, I don't know. A pie made of sausage."

Molly wrinkles her nose.

"Carrying my canoe between bodies of water? I've never been one for boating." Vivian shakes her head. "What's it supposed to mean, exactly?"

The idea of portaging seemed clear when Mr. Reed was explaining it, but now Molly's not so sure herself. "Maybe I could just ask some of the questions on my list," she suggests.

"Well, I suppose you can try."

They are sitting in the red wingback chairs in the living room, their work in the attic finished for the day. Vivian calls for Terry, saying that she needs a cup of tea and that Molly does too.

After a few minutes Terry brings them the tea in thick white mugs. Vivian stirs sugar into hers and pushes the bowl over to Molly. Molly has never really liked tea that much, but she stirs in the sugar and tries a sip. Not bad. It warms her from the inside out.

She pushes down the button on the tiny digital recorder that she signed out from the library at school, takes a deep breath, and asks Vivian her first question.

"So, have you ever gone on a big trip in your life? I mean, moved from one place to another?"

Vivian, who was raising the mug of tea toward her lips, seems to change her mind. She sets it down on a small table by her chair. "Yes," she says. "Certainly."

Molly waits a few seconds, but Vivian doesn't say any more.

"From where to where?" Molly asks.

Vivian looks at the recorder in Molly's hand a little warily, as if it might hiss or bite. "Well, when I was young my family moved from Galway—that's in Ireland— to New York City. But I took an even bigger journey a few years later."

"From where to where?" Molly prompts again.

"From New York to Minnesota. On a train."

NIAMH
ALBANS, MINNESOTA, 1929

As the train pulled up to the depot, Niamh could see that the town of Albans was barely a town at all. There was no station, just a platform open to the wind and sun. The children who hadn't been chosen in Minneapolis were herded in a line toward the Grange Hall, a block from the station.

This time there was no stage, so Niamh and the other children walked to the front of a large, bare room and turned to face the crowd. What would happen if no one wanted her here, either? She'd go on to the other stops, maybe back to New York and the orphanage. That might not be so bad. She knew what to expect there— hard mattresses, rough sheets, strict matrons. But also other girls to live with, three meals a day, school. It was probably better than what Dutchy was facing.

A woman came closer, her eyes on Niamh. She had wavy brown hair cropped close to her head, a plain white blouse, and a dark paisley scarf. There was a large oval locket on a gold chain around her neck. Seeing it, Niamh reached up and touched her own necklace.

The man standing behind the woman was stout and red-faced, with shaggy auburn hair. The buttons of his waistcoat strained across his stomach.

"What's your name?" the woman asked.

"Niamh," she said, her voice almost lost in the noise of footsteps, coughs and sneezes, mutters and whispering.

"Eve?"

"No, Niamh. It's Irish," she says.

"The name would have to change," the woman said to her husband.

"Whatever you want, m'dear."

She cocked her head at Niamh. "How old are you?"

"Nine, ma'am."

"Can you sew?"

Niamh nodded.

"Do you know how to cross-stitch? Hem? Can you do backstitching by hand?"

"Yes, ma'am," Niamh said. She used to help her mother when she took in extra work darning and mending.

The woman nodded at the man, who put his hand on her back and guided her to the side of the room. Niamh watched as they talked. He shook his head. She gestured toward Niamh. He stooped and bent close to whisper in her ear. She looked Niamh up and down.

Then the two came back over.

"I am Mrs. Byrne," the woman said. "We employ several women, making clothes to order. We are looking for a girl who is good with a needle."

Niamh didn't know what to say. She was good at sewing, better than other girls her age. At least that's what her mam had said. But she didn't know if she wanted to announce this. She didn't know if she wanted to go with this grim woman. If she didn't, though, somebody worse might come along.

"I will be honest with you. We do not have any

children and we have no interest in becoming parents," the woman said stiffly. "But if you are respectful and hardworking, you will be treated fairly."

Niamh nodded to show she understood.

"Good," Mrs. Byrne said. She shook Niamh's hand, as if they'd just made a business deal. Somehow, Niamh realized, she had already agreed to go with these people.

Once the paperwork was done, Niamh followed the Byrnes out to their car, a black Model A. Mr. Byrne opened the rear door for her. The leather seats were cool and slippery. The two adults took their places in the front and didn't look back. With a loud rumble the car sprang to life. Niamh could see that the Byrnes were talking in the front seat, but she couldn't hear a word over the noise of the engine.

Several minutes later, Mr. Byrne pulled into the driveway of a small, beige house. As soon as he turned off the car, Mrs. Byrne looked back at Niamh and said, "We've decided on Dorothy."

It took a moment for Niamh to realize what she meant.

"You like that name?" Mr. Byrne asked.

"For goodness' sake, Raymond, it doesn't matter what she thinks," Mrs. Byrne snapped as she opened her car door. "Dorothy is our choice, and Dorothy she will be."

MOLLY
SPRUCE HARBOR, MAINE, PRESENT DAY

One of the things Molly likes most about Spruce Harbor is the Island Explorer bus. It's free, and it makes one big loop around Mount Desert Island. Molly can get on the bus after she's finished at Vivian's, get off about fifteen minutes later, and then it's just a short walk down the main street of Spruce Harbor to Ralph and Dina's.

This time, on her way back, Molly stops to look in the window of the thrift shop. A T-shirt catches her eye. Tie-dyed, with colorful turtles splashed across the front. Their shells, deep blues and rich greens, remind Molly of little planets, spinning in space.

But it's not black. When is the last time Molly bought a piece of clothing that wasn't black?

She stands there, looking, and in the glass of the window she sees a reflection from across the street. It's Megan, from social studies, walking with two other girls Molly doesn't know. They're all laughing at some joke. Megan's bright hair, gold with a touch of red, swings out as she clutches one of her friend's arms and points across the street.

"Let's check out the thrift store!" she says, loud enough for Molly to hear.

Molly stuffs her hands into her pockets and starts

walking fast, away from Megan and her friends, before they can see her standing there alone.

NIAMH
ALBANS, MINNESOTA, 1929

Niamh—who couldn't imagine how she was going to think of herself as Dorothy—followed the Byrnes inside the house, into a small front hallway, gloomy and dark. Shadows from the white crocheted curtains on every window cast lacy shapes on the floor.

To the left, through an open doorway, Niamh could see red-flocked wallpaper, a shiny wooden table and chairs. A dining room. Then Mrs. Byrne opened the door to the right onto a room that, to Niamh's surprise, was full of people.

Two women in white blouses sat in front of black sewing machines with the word *Singer* spelled out in gold, each pumping one foot on the pedal underneath. Niamh stared, fascinated, as the needles on the machines moved up and down. She'd heard of sewing machines, but never seen one up close.

A young woman with frizzy brown hair knelt on the floor in front of a cloth mannequin, stitching tiny pearls on a bodice. A gray-haired woman perched on a brown chair, hemming a calico skirt. And a girl who seemed to be only a few years older than Niamh sat at a table, cutting a pattern out of thin paper.

Mrs. Byrne looked around the room. "As you know, we've needed extra help for quite some time, and I am pleased to report that we have found it. This is Dorothy." She lifted her hand in Niamh's direction. "Dorothy, say hello to Bernice"—the woman with the frizzy hair—"Joan and Sally"—the women at the sewing machines—"Fanny"—the gray-haired woman, the only one who smiled—"and Mary." This was the young girl with the scissors, who barely glanced up, only to return to her work with an angry face. "Mary, you will help Dorothy get familiar with her tasks. She can take over some of yours. Fanny, you will oversee. As always."

"Yes, ma'am," Fanny said.

"Well, then," Mrs. Byrne said. "Let's get back to work."

And she left.

Niamh spent the next few hours doing jobs no one else wanted to do: basting garments together with quick, large stitches so that one of the older women could finish them with finer work later; sweeping; collecting pins and putting them in pincushions. After a while she was forced to speak up. "Excuse me. I need the lavatory," she said to Mary. "Can you tell me where it is?"

Mary looked annoyed, but before she could answer, Fanny got to her feet. "Reckon I'll take her." Niamh followed her into a spare and spotless kitchen and out the back door to an outhouse.

"I'll wait," Fanny said.

"You don't have to," Niamh told her.

"The longer you're in there, the longer my fingers can have a rest."

The shed was drafty. Strips of newspaper hung on a roll on the wall. Niamh had used a privy back home in Ireland, so the smell didn't shock her, but she couldn't help wondering what it would be like out here in a snowstorm. When she was finished, she opened the door, pulling down her dress.

"You're pitiful thin," Fanny said. "I'll bet you're hungry."

She was right. Niamh's stomach felt hollow. "A little," she admitted.

"Mrs. Byrne don't give us much for meals, but it's probably more than you had." Fanny reached into a side pocket of her dress, neatly made of cotton printed with purple flowers. She pulled out a small shiny apple.

"I always save something for later. She locks up the refrigerator between meals." She handed over the apple.

"I don't want to—" Niamh hesitated.

"Go ahead. You got to learn to take what people are willing to give."

The apple smelled so fresh that Niamh's mouth watered. She reached out a hand for it and Fanny nodded.

"You best eat it here, before we go back in," she advised. In a few bites, Niamh devoured the apple down to the core. Juice ran down her chin, and she wiped it with her hand and then licked the sticky sweetness off her skin.

"Why doesn't Mary like me?" she asked, her mouth still tingling with the taste of the apple.

"Pish. It isn't that she doesn't like you, child. She's scared."

Niamh blinked, astonished. "Of me?"

"She thinks you're going to take her job," Fanny said. "Mrs. Byrne holds her money tight in her fist. Why would she pay Mary to do the work you can be trained to do for nothing?"

Now it was clear: Niamh was little more than slave labor. "I'm the only one who isn't paid?"

Fanny's smile was kind. "You can see why Mary

would be threatened. And she knows you're good with a needle. Come now, or we'll be missed."

That night at supper Mrs. Byrne served chopped beef, potato salad stained pink by beets, and rubbery cabbage. Niamh was so hungry by then that it felt as if something was clawing at her stomach from the inside, but she forced herself to put her napkin in her lap and take small bites.

No one spoke until Mrs. Byrne put down her fork and said, "Dorothy, it's time to discuss the rules of the house. You'll use the privy in the back. Once a week, on Sunday evenings, I will draw a bath for you in the washroom off the kitchen. Bedtime is at nine p.m., with lights out. There's a pallet for you in the hall closet. You'll bring it out in the evening and roll it up neatly in the morning, before the girls arrive at eight thirty."

Niamh was startled into speech. "I'm sleeping in the hallway?"

"Mercy, you don't expect to sleep on the second floor with us?" Mrs. Byrne said with a laugh. "Heaven forbid."

After dinner, Mr. Byrne went for a stroll. Mrs. Byrne said that she had work to do upstairs. Niamh was left with the dishes. By the time she finished scrubbing and drying and had wiped down the counter, the clock above the stove said 7:30.

She poured herself a glass of water from the tap and sat down at the table.

It felt too early to go to bed, but she didn't know what else to do. She wished she had a book to read. At home in New York there weren't many books in the house, but the twins were always bringing home day-old newspapers, and they'd puzzle out the stories. Or she might recite a poem she'd learned in school. She closed her eyes and whispered, "All that we see or seem / Is but a dream within a dream." But that was all she could remember.

It's not so bad here, she told herself. The Byrnes weren't particularly kind, maybe, but they didn't seem cruel. They didn't want to be her family, but perhaps that was for the best. Carmine might be happy with his new mam, but he was just a baby, ready to love anyone with gentle arms and a smile. Niamh was no infant. With the Byrnes, she'd have food, a place to sleep, work to do—perhaps that was enough. And soon she would go to school.

She'd have a better life than poor Dutchy, she thought.

She found her suitcase in the hall closet, along with a pile of bedding. She unrolled a horsehair pallet and put a thin, yellow pillow at the top. There was a white sheet and a moth-eaten quilt.

When her bed was settled, she visited the privy outside. On her way back in, she noticed that some-one—Mrs. Byrne, it must've been—had come into the kitchen while she was gone. There was now a padlock on the refrigerator door.

Chapter Nine

MOLLY
SPRUCE HARBOR, MAINE, PRESENT DAY

It's Monday, but there's no school. It's a teacher enrichment day. Ralph and Dina are at work. Jack's playing soccer with some friends. And Molly doesn't feel like spending the entire day alone at home.

She figures she might as well head over to Vivian's and get some of her hours done. She's been going there on her own for a couple of weeks already. She'll catch the bus back and be home again before Ralph or Dina get off work. She'll bring the tape recorder, too; it's still in her backpack. Maybe she can ask Vivian a few more questions.

At Vivian's, Molly rings the bell, but nobody answers. Cupping her hands against the glass, she peers into the dim hallway.

Vivian never goes out, does she? Molly tries the doorknob. It turns.

"Hello?" she says as she steps inside.

Maybe Vivian can't hear her. Molly walks down the hall and hesitantly looks into the living room.

The shades are closed. Vivian isn't there. Should Molly leave? Without any voices to listen to, the old house is full of noises—floors creaking, windowpanes rattling, flies buzzing, curtains flapping. She can smell old books and something savory from the kitchen. Terry must be in there cooking.

Molly is looking at the books on a bookshelf when a door opens—she glimpses the kitchen on the other side—and Terry bustles in.

Molly turns. "Uh, hi."

Terry shrieks, clutching the rag she's holding to her chest. "What are you doing here?"

"I-I rang the bell a few times," Molly stammers. "I just kind of let myself in. I thought—"

"Does Vivian know you're coming this early?"

"Not really. I just—there's no school, and I—"

Terry narrows her eyes and frowns. "There's no school. That doesn't mean you can just show up here whenever you feel like it."

Molly can feel her face getting warm. "I know. I just—I'm sorry."

"Vivian has a routine. Gets up at eight or nine,

comes downstairs at ten. But that's not the point. You broke in."

She didn't! All she did was turn the handle! "That's not—"

But Terry doesn't let Molly finish. "And another thing," she goes on. "I was in the attic this morning. Are you actually getting anything *done* up there?"

"Vivian doesn't want to get rid of anything," Molly says. Her heartbeat is starting to quicken. What is Terry saying? That she thinks Molly's not doing what she's supposed to be doing?

Terry puts the hand holding the dishrag on her hip. "I let Jack talk me into suggesting this to Vivian. Don't ask me why. A kid like you . . . Listen. If you can't finish the job—"

"I'm doing my best!" Molly says.

Terry shakes her head. "If you can't get this done, I'm the one who's going to look bad to Vivian. Do you get that? Or are you just thinking about yourself?"

Molly is shocked to feel hot tears suddenly pressing behind her eyes. She doesn't cry. She never cries. She's certainly not going to cry in front of Terry. She looks past her, focusing hard on a shiny blue vase sitting on a table, and wills the tears away.

Any words she might say to Terry are squashed to

nothing in her throat. She can tell it won't do any good to object to the unfairness. Terry's already decided that Molly is worthless. A slacker. A thief.

A kid like you.

Terry sighs. "Look. I don't mean to be hard on you. Jack likes you. Just get the attic done, all right? And no more walking in here without permission. Got it?"

Molly nods, still looking hard at the vase. There are purple flowers in it, and tall sprays of something white and feathery.

"I guess, now that you're here, we can see if Vivian wants to get something done upstairs," Terry goes on. "But you'll have to wait for her to come down. I'm not going to go upstairs and hurry her. And I've got my own work to do. I suppose you can stay in here." She heads back to the kitchen, leaving the door open behind her.

Molly sinks into a chair. She looks around at the bookshelves, but she doesn't dare to pull out a book— Terry probably thinks Molly would steal any book she gets her hands on.

The book Vivian gave to Molly is still in her backpack. Well, at least that's one thing that's been cleaned out of the attic! Molly pulls it out and opens it to the first page.

The neat lines of letters on the page soothe her. She

feels her heartbeat slow down as she settles into the book. Let somebody else's troubles fill her mind for a while—troubles she can close the cover on and set aside when she's done.

The sun moves higher in the sky and the room brightens as Molly reads about old Matthew Cuthbert going somewhere in his buggy, and nosy Mrs. Lynde, just dying of curiosity. Mrs. Lynde reminds her of Terry. The idea makes her smile. *"Are you actually getting anything done up there?"* It's something Mrs. Lynde might say, for sure. She turns the page and Matthew is at the train station, meeting a girl. An orphan who needs a home.

The Cuthberts don't want a girl—they want a boy. A boy to help with the farmwork. But instead they get a red-haired girl who talks too much and isn't what they need.

Not what they signed up for, in fact.

After a little while, the door to the hall opens, and Molly looks up. Vivian comes in, glances around the room, focuses on Molly, and smiles.

"Bright and early!" she says. "Maybe I'll let you empty out a box today. Or two, if you're lucky. Maybe I'll even answer some questions for that canoeing paper of yours. Now, let's have a cup of tea."

On a Monday morning, after she'd been at the Byrnes' for five days, Niamh got up early and washed her face in the kitchen sink. She braided her hair carefully and attached two ribbons she'd found in the scrap pile in the sewing room. Then she put on her cleanest dress and her pinafore.

At breakfast—lumpy oatmeal with no sugar—she asked the Byrnes how to get to school.

Mrs. Byrne looked at her husband, then back at Niamh. "Dorothy, Mr. Byrne and I feel that you are not ready for school."

Niamh looked at Mr. Byrne, studiously tying his shoelace. "But I'm supposed to go," she said.

"The timing is unfortunate," Mrs. Byrne said. "School has been in session for a month. You are impossibly behind, with no chance of catching up this year."

Niamh's skin prickled. "But . . . Mrs. Scatcherd said—"

"Mrs. Scatcherd isn't here now, is she? We're the ones who decide what's best for you. And we think you should wait. Lord knows what your schooling was like in the slum."

"I wasn't in a—slum," she choked out. "I was in the

fourth grade. My teacher was Miss Uhrig. I was in the chorus, and we did an operetta. 'Polished Pebbles.'"

They both looked at her. This was the longest speech Niamh had made in their house yet.

"I like school," she said.

Mrs. Byrne got up and started to stack the dishes, taking Niamh's plate, even though she hadn't finished her toast.

"You insolent girl. I don't want to hear another word," she said. "Is that clear?"

The subject of school never came up again.

Mr. Byrne always left the house after breakfast, though Niamh was never sure exactly what he did while he was gone. Niamh would go into the sewing room once she'd finished washing the dishes. Several times a day Mrs. Byrne would appear there. But she never picked up a needle. She inspected what had been sewn, handed out new orders, and collected the finished garments.

There were many rules in the Byrnes' household. Niamh learned about them mostly by breaking them and being scolded for it. Her bed linen had to be folded neatly each morning. The doors were supposed to be shut, unless someone was actually coming or going. Niamh was not to be in the kitchen at all, except if she was washing dishes or cleaning up after a meal.

She didn't help cook—maybe because Mrs. Byrne was afraid that she'd steal food.

Mrs. Byrne served soft gray peas from a can, starchy boiled potatoes, watery stews. The food tasted awful, but at the same time, there was never enough, and Niamh almost always felt a dull ache of hunger. Like Fanny, she slipped an apple or a piece of bread into her pocket whenever she could.

As the weather got colder, the leaves on the trees turned from rose-tinged to candy-apple red to a dull brown. One day Mrs. Byrne looked Niamh up and down and asked if she had any other clothes.

Niamh glanced at her blue-and-white-checked dress, the one she'd been given at the orphanage. "Just the brown gingham. Ma'am." She'd been wearing the blue dress one day, the brown one the next, day after day.

"Well, then," Mrs. Byrne said. "You will make yourself some."

Later that afternoon she drove Niamh to the general store.

"You may choose three different fabrics," she said. "Let's see—three yards each. The cloth must be sturdy and inexpensive."

Mrs. Byrne led Niamh over to a section filled with bolts of fabric, nodding at the cheaper ones. Niamh chose a blue-and-gray-checked cotton, a delicate green print, and a pink paisley. Mrs. Byrne nodded at the first two choices but grimaced at the third. "Mercy, not with red hair." She pulled out a bolt of blue chambray. "Do you have a coat? Or a sweater?" she asked.

Niamh thought about the too-small coat in her suitcase and shook her head.

After the fabric was measured, cut, wrapped in brown paper, and tied with twine, Niamh followed Mrs. Byrne down the street to a different shop, full of clothes already made. Mrs. Byrne headed straight for the sale rack at the back and found a mustard-colored wool coat with black buttons, several sizes too big. "Well, it's a good deal," she said. "And there's no sense in getting something you'll outgrow in a month."

Niamh hated the coat. The color was dreadful, and it was scratchy and rough and not even very warm. No wonder it had ended up in the back of the store, on the remainder rack. But she was afraid to say no. It was going to get colder soon, and if she objected, Mrs. Byrne might not get her a coat at all.

"Thank you, ma'am."

"You're welcome. And because we saved money on the coat, I can get you something else." Mrs. Byrne pulled two sweaters off the clearance rack, one navy blue and one off-white.

Back at the house, standing in front of the hall mirror

in her new blue sweater, Niamh found that the clothes made it easier, somehow, to answer to her new name. She wasn't the same Niamh who left her gram and aunties and uncles in Ireland and came across the ocean on the *Agnes Pauline*, who'd lived with her family on Elizabeth Street, who'd sat on a bench in a rattling train with Dutchy and Carmine by her side.

No. She was Dorothy now.

Chapter Ten

MOLLY
SPRUCE HARBOR, MAINE, PRESENT DAY

"How about this?" Molly holds up a shabby quilt with a pattern of rings, all linked together. "You don't need this anymore, right?"

"Just fold it again and put it on that pile," Vivian says, pointing to a stack of things Molly's already taken out of the cedar chest.

Molly groans inside. How is she supposed to convince Terry that she's really doing work up here if Vivian won't get rid of anything? The chest is empty, and the only things Vivian let her put in a garbage bag were a few old towels.

Molly folds the quilt and plops it on the floor. As she bends down she sees that the chest isn't quite empty after all. She reaches into the back corner and pulls out a roll of thin, loosely woven cloth that must've once been white. Obviously not worth saving. She reaches for the garbage bag.

"Gracious," Vivian says from her seat on a box. "I had no idea that was in there. Give it to me."

"But we have to get rid of some things," Molly protests.

Vivian reaches over to take the cloth out of Molly's hand. "Don't be so hasty. You have to look at everything carefully." She unrolls the bundle. Several things fall onto her lap—a round red pincushion bristling with pins, two spools of thread, a small pair of scissors, and a packet of needles. Buttons patter down like rain.

"There, you see?" Vivian scoops up a handful.

Molly sighs. "So we're keeping all this?"

"I'll make you a bargain," Vivian says. "You can throw the cheesecloth away if you find me another bag or box for the sewing supplies."

Molly shakes her head, rummages in the pile of things she just removed from the cedar chest, and turns up a small wooden box. "Will this do?"

"Excellent." Vivian piles the needles and thread into the box, tucking the pincushion into a corner. "Someone could still get some use out of those. Like you, perhaps. Do you sew?"

Molly laughs. Does Vivian think she sits around doing embroidery? "What would I sew?"

"I don't know. Clothes, perhaps. Your trousers are ripped, there on the knee. Wouldn't you like to know how to sew that up? Or if you lose a button on a shirt, what do you do?"

Molly looks down at her jeans and her T-shirt, black with a silver rose stenciled on the front. "I don't have any shirts with buttons. And I like my jeans ripped. Anyway, I got them at the thrift store. I can get another pair if I need to."

Vivian shakes her head. "Young people today. Wearing ripped clothing on purpose. Throwing things out when they're a little worn. It wasn't that way when I was growing up. We patched things up," Vivian goes on. "We made do. We didn't have a choice."

Molly doesn't like being lectured. But she's curious enough to let go of her annoyance. Vivian wasn't always rich? "Are you talking about when you lived in Ireland?" she asks. She starts to put things back in the cedar chest, setting neatly folded blankets on the bottom, picking up the quilt to put on top of them. "Or later, when you were in Minnesota?"

"I certainly did plenty of sewing in Minnesota," Vivian says with an odd little snort. "Wait. Let me see that quilt again."

Molly holds it out. The cotton batting inside shows

through a few holes, and the colors are no longer bright—purples have faded to pinks and lavenders, yellows almost white.

"I think this could go on one of the beds downstairs," Vivian says. "Instead of back in that chest."

It's not quite as good as throwing it away, Molly thinks, but at least it's something. Something to show Terry that she *is* doing work up here. And the quilt is still pretty, still warm. Maybe Vivian's right—it would be a shame to get rid of it just because it isn't perfect.

"So what kind of sewing did you do in Minnesota?" she asks. She picks up the notebook that Terry gave her. She's been using it to write a list of what's inside every box, but it could have another use as well. The recorder is downstairs, in her backpack, so she flips to a clean page of the notebook, ready to scribble down the things Vivian tells her.

"Dresses, mostly."

"For yourself?"

"Well, I did make myself a few things to wear," Vivian says. "But mostly I sewed for others. Until—well, until no one wanted to buy dresses anymore."

"Why didn't they?"

"Because there came a time when it wasn't just poor Irish immigrants who had to learn to manage with what they had, or do without. Everyone had to make do."

DOROTHY
ALBANS, MINNESOTA, 1929

One quiet Tuesday afternoon, shortly after Dorothy had finished sewing one of her new dresses, Mrs. Byrne appeared in the sewing room. It was clear at once that something was wrong. She looked stricken. Her short dark bob, usually in tight waves against her head, stuck out all over. Fanny jumped up, but Mrs. Byrne waved her away.

"Girls," she said, holding her hand to her throat, "I need to tell you something! The stock market crashed today."

Dorothy didn't know what the stock market was. Later Fanny would tell her that she wasn't sure herself, but she thought it was something like a bank, a place rich people keep their money. And if it crashed, well, it was like a bank failing. The money was just gone.

"Some people are losing everything," Mrs. Byrne muttered, gripping the back of Mary's chair. "If we can't feed ourselves, we can hardly afford to pay you, can we?" She backed out of the room, shaking her head.

Dorothy heard the front door open and Mrs. Byrne clatter down the steps.

Slowly, over the next few days, Dorothy came to understand more about what had happened. Mr. Byrne had invested a good deal of his money in the stock market, and that money had vanished. Other people, who had also lost money, were not ordering new clothes. They were making their own, repairing what they had, or doing without.

Weeks went by. Dorothy and the women finished up the dresses they had on hand, but new orders were slow to come. And outside, snow began to fall.

Dorothy was astonished by the cold. In Kinvara, winters were cold and gray and wet. In New York they were slushy and miserable. But here, her fingers grew so stiff that she had to stop and rub them so that she could keep sewing.

At the end of the workday on Christmas Eve, Fanny slipped Dorothy a small brown-wrapped parcel. "Open this later," she whispered. "Tell them you brought it from home."

Dorothy waded out to the privy through snowdrifts and opened the package there. It held a pair of thick brown wool mittens. She clutched them tightly to her chest, warmed by Fanny's kindness as well as the heavy wool.

One day in January, Mrs. Byrne came into the sewing room and asked Sally, Joan, and Bernice to step out into the hall. Several minutes later, they returned, picked up their belongings in silence, and left.

It was a windy afternoon in early March when Mrs. Byrne slipped into the room and asked for Mary. Dorothy felt sorry for the girl, despite her sour looks. This was what Mary had been afraid of, all along, and it had happened at last.

A week later, the doorbell rang. Fanny and Dorothy looked at each other in surprise. In all her time in that house, Dorothy had never heard the doorbell ring.

They heard Mrs. Byrne rustle down the stairs. They heard her talking to a man in the hall.

The door to the sewing room opened, and in came a heavyset man in a black felt hat and a gray suit. He had a black mustache and jowls like a basset hound.

"This the girl?" he asked, pointing a sausage finger at Dorothy.

Mrs. Byrne nodded.

The man took off his hat and set it on a small table by the door. He pulled a piece of paper out of one pocket and a pair of eyeglasses out of another. "Let's see. Nem Power?"

It took Dorothy a moment to realize that he was trying to say her old name. "I'm Dorothy now."

He looked over his glasses at Mrs. Byrne. "You changed her name to Dorothy?"

"We thought the girl should have an American name," Mrs. Byrne said.

"And you did not change her surname."

"Of course not."

"You weren't considering adoption?"

"Mercy, no."

The clock ticked loudly over the mantelpiece. The man folded up the piece of paper and put it in his pocket.

"Dorothy, I am Mr. Sorenson," he said. "I'm a local agent of the Children's Aid Society, and I oversee the placement of the train riders. Oftentimes the placements work out as they should, and everyone is content. But sometimes it's necessary . . . that is . . . we need to find new accommodations. Do you understand?"

Dorothy nodded, although she didn't know what "accommodations" meant. Mrs. Byrne drifted over to the window. She pulled aside the lace curtain and stared out into the street.

"Good. There's a couple in Hemingford—well, on a farm outside of town, actually—who've requested a girl your age. A mother, father, and four children. Wilma and Gerald Grote."

Dorothy turned to Mrs. Byrne. "You don't want me anymore?"

Although she knew quite well that as far as Mrs. Byrne was concerned, she was nothing more than a hand to hold a needle, Dorothy was shocked. This hadn't been a kind home, or a welcoming home, but it had been a home. And now? Where would she go?

"It's a complicated situation," Mr. Sorenson said.

With a sudden movement, Mrs. Byrne dropped the curtain and wheeled around. "She eats too much!" she cried. "I have to lock up the refrigerator! We bought her clothes, so many clothes! Gave her a place to sleep—and it's not enough! It's never enough!"

She put her palms over her eyes and ran out into the hallway and up the stairs, slamming the door at the top.

The three people left in the room were silent. Dorothy felt ashamed, somehow, as if she'd done wrong—but what? Mrs. Byrne had padlocked the refrigerator long before she arrived. But would Mr. Sorenson believe what he'd just been told? Think of her as greedy and ungrateful?

"That woman ought to be ashamed," Fanny said firmly. "The girl is nothing but skin and bones. They never even sent her to school."

Hot tears prickled behind Dorothy's eyes, and she gave Fanny a quick, grateful smile.

Mr. Sorenson cleared his throat. "Well," he says, "perhaps this will be for the best. The Grotes are good country people, from what I hear."

"And they have four children?" Dorothy asked shakily. "Why do they want another?"

"As I understand it—and I could be wrong; I haven't

had the pleasure to meet them yet—Mrs. Grote is once again with child, and she is looking for a mother's helper."

Dorothy thought of Carmine. With a tightening in her throat, she thought of Maisie. She imagined a tidy white farmhouse with black shutters, a red barn in the back, plump chickens in a coop. Maybe it would be like that. "When do they want me?"

"I'm taking you there now," Mr. Sorenson said.

Fanny watched as Dorothy packed her brown suitcase, putting in the new dresses and sweaters along with her old ones from the Children's Aid and the warm brown mittens. She was tempted to leave the ugly, mustard-colored coat behind, but Fanny shook her head.

"It's even colder out on those farms than it is here in town," she said. "You'll need that coat, believe me."

Dorothy put on the coat and carefully tucked Dutchy's penny into a pocket, buttoning it tight so that the coin couldn't fall out.

Then Fanny beckoned her back into the sewing room. The older woman gathered up a pair of scissors, two spools of thread, a pincushion and pins, and a packet of needles. She added several gleaming white buttons and wrapped it all in cheesecloth for Dorothy to slip into her suitcase.

"Won't you get in trouble?" Dorothy asked.

"Pish," Fanny said. "I don't even care."

Dorothy didn't try to say good-bye to Mrs. Byrne. But she gave Fanny a long hug, and Fanny held her face in her small, cold hands. "You are a good girl, Niamh," she whispered. "Don't let anybody tell you different."

The girl nodded, not sure who she was for that moment—Niamh or Dorothy or someone else altogether? A good girl, or one nobody would ever want? She hugged Fanny again and said good-bye. Then she told Mr. Sorenson she was ready to go.

Chapter Eleven

MOLLY
SPRUCE HARBOR, MAINE, PRESENT DAY

"So," Lori says as Molly drops her brown lunch bag on one of the tables in the science lab. "You're letting that blue stripe in your hair grow out?"

Molly shrugs. It's getting to be a pain, remembering to bleach and dye it. She likes the stripe, likes the way it makes everybody look at her twice and then away, likes how it makes her seem as different on the outside as she feels on the inside. But now that she thinks about it, maybe looking different hasn't seemed so important to her lately.

"And you've done about ten hours of your community service, right?" Lori watches Molly take her sandwich out of her bag. "What's it like? And please don't say 'fine.' Tell me something interesting."

Molly shakes her head and laughs a little.

Lori smiles. "We need to have these conversations,

you and me," she says. "They don't actually have to be boring. It's not a law."

Boring? Molly never really thought she was being boring. Is that what Lori thinks? But when she runs her mind over the conversations they've had week after week, she can see why Lori might think so.

"Not bad," she says tentatively. "Better than I thought it would be, actually."

"Better how?"

"It's just . . . interesting."

"Tell me one interesting thing. As a favor. Please?"

Molly hesitates, thinking. "Yesterday there was an old quilt. It was kind of pretty. And a box of Christmas ornaments too. Really old, like seventy years old. Vivian told me about how she used to decorate the store for the holidays, her family's department store. They'd put a pine tree in the window, a real one, and Vivian would hang up the ornaments." That's all Molly says, but she can remember the ornaments now as she sits in Lori's office, cardboard stars and snowflakes covered in gold and silver glitter, red and green and golden balls made out of glass. Molly liked lifting them out of the boxes one by one, handling them gently, thinking of all the years they'd been hidden away.

Lori nods. She actually seems interested. "That's

cool. I wish I could see them." She flips through papers in a file. "You're doing well, Molly. Mrs. Creech says you've raised your hand a couple of times in Language Arts. And your grades in math have come up."

"It's an easy school," Molly mutters.

"It isn't, actually." Lori flaps the folder shut. "Bring me something interesting to talk about next week too, okay?"

"No promises. Next week we'll probably be back to boring."

Lori smiles. "For some reason I doubt that."

DOROTHY
HEMINGFORD COUNTY, MINNESOTA, 1930

Mr. Sorenson held the door of a dark-green Chrysler truck open for Dorothy. They drove away from town, in a direction Dorothy had never been.

Soon there were fields all around, a dull brown patchwork. Cows huddling together lifted their necks to watch the noisy truck. Mr. Sorenson told her about the fields they were passing: grain, sugar beets, sweet corn, green peas.

Dorothy smiled and nodded, though she was barely listening. *This is what I have to do,* she thought. *I have to pretend. Smile and nod and try to act like everybody else, even though I feel broken inside.*

Did she feel broken because she had no family anymore? Or did no new family want her because she was broken? It was hard to know. Either way, she was quite sure that the brokenness was something to hide.

After about half an hour, Mr. Sorenson turned onto a narrow unpaved road. They passed more fields and crossed a dilapidated bridge over a murky stream. Then they turned down a bumpy road lined with pine trees. Branches scraped the car on either side.

After about fifty yards, they came to a small wooden house. A shack, really—unpainted, with a sagging front porch piled with junk.

On a bare patch of ground in front of the house, a toddler was crawling on top of a dog with black matted fur. A boy of about six poked a stick into the dirt. It was icy cold, but both children were barefoot.

Mr. Sorenson parked the truck and they got out. "Hello, boy," he said to the older one.

The child gaped at him, not answering.

"Your mama home?" he asked. "Did she tell you you're getting a new sister?"

"No."

"Well, she should be expecting us. Go on and tell her we're here."

The boy stabbed at the dirt with a stick. "She's sleeping. I'm not to bother her."

"You go on and wake her up. Maybe she forgot we were coming."

The boy traced a circle in the dirt. When it became clear that he wasn't going to move, Mr. Sorenson rubbed his hands together and, motioning for Dorothy to follow, made his way up the creaking front steps to the porch.

He knocked loudly, and the door swung open. He stepped into the gloom inside. Dorothy followed, her dream of a snug white farmhouse with black shutters melting away like sugar in hot tea.

The front room was nearly bare. A wooden crate stood between two chairs, and an ancient sofa spilled stuffing out of its split seams. On the far left was a dark hallway. Straight ahead, through an open doorway, Dorothy could see a grimy kitchen.

"Mrs. Grote?" Mr. Sorenson called.

They heard faint footsteps and a girl of about three, in a dirty pink dress, made her way out of the hall. A harsh voice came from the darker end. "What do you want?"

A moment later a pale woman with long brown hair, wearing a nightgown, stepped out of the darkness. The girl slipped over like a cat and wrapped herself around the woman's legs.

"I'm Chester Sorenson from the Children's Aid Society. You must be Mrs. Grote. I'm sorry to bother you, ma'am, but I was told you knew we were coming. You did request a girl, did you not?"

The woman rubbed her eyes. "What day is it?"

"Friday, March fourth, ma'am. Now, is Mr. Grote home?"

She shook her head.

"Are you expecting him soon?"

She lifted her shoulders in a shrug. "I'm just so tired," she muttered.

"Well, I'm sure you are, ma'am." It was clear that Mr. Sorenson was itching to leave. He would go soon, Dorothy was sure, and she would be left here, in this filthy place, with this woman who didn't want her, who hadn't even looked at her yet. "I'm guessing," Mr. Sorenson said, as if he was hoping to wake Mrs. Grote up a little, "that's why you asked for this here orphan girl. Dorothy. Her papers say she has experience with children."

At last Mrs. Grote focused on Dorothy's face. "What's her age?"

"Nine years old."

"I have enough kids," she said, shaking her head. "What I need is somebody who can help me out."

"It's all part of the deal," Mr. Sorenson explained.

"You feed and clothe Dorothy and make sure she goes to school. I'm told there's a school four miles from here. And there's a ride she can catch at the post road. It's required that Dorothy attend school, Mrs. Grote. Do you agree to abide by that?"

The front door creaked open. They all turned to see a tall, thin, dark-haired man wearing a plaid shirt and grungy overalls.

"Of course this girl will go to school, whether she wants to or not," he said. "I'll make sure of it." He nodded at Dorothy. "She'll do just fine."

There was paperwork, but not a lot. A few minutes later, Mr. Sorenson brought Dorothy's suitcase inside and bid them all good day. Dorothy watched him go through the cracked front window as a thin, high crying arose from the bedroom where Mrs. Grote had been asleep.

Mrs. Grote disappeared into the bedroom and returned with a baby in her arms. "This is Nettie," she said, thrusting the child at Dorothy. "See if you can settle her down." She headed back toward the bedroom, and Dorothy jostled the little girl and then rocked her, trying to quiet her. Nettie put her head on Dorothy's shoulder, her crying softening into a fretful whine.

Mr. Grote watched the two of them. "Where will I sleep?" Dorothy asked him.

He looked at her, hands on his hips, as if he hadn't considered such a thing. Then he waved a hand toward the dark hallway. "There's a bedroom yonder," he said. "If you don't want to sleep with the others, I guess you can stay on the couch. We don't stand on ceremony here."

Dorothy walked down the hall to the bedroom and opened the door. Three old mattresses with no sheets had been laid across the floor. The older children, Mabel, Gerald Jr., and Harold, sprawled across them, tugging a tattered wool blanket and several old quilts from one another.

It was hard for Dorothy to believe she might end up in a place worse than the Byrnes', but she was beginning to realize she had.

Over the next few days she came to understand just how much worse. There was no heat, running water, or electricity. They used gas lamps and candles for light and the hearth for warmth, though the damp logs in the fireplace gave off more smoke than heat. As there had been at the Byrnes, there was an outhouse in the back.

Mrs. Grote slept most of the time in the other bedroom, which was as dark as a cave, with brown paper tacked over the broken window. Something was wrong with her, Dorothy could tell. Was she ill? Was she just too tired to take care of the children, wash her clothes, comb her hair? Dorothy stayed away from the woman as much as she could, which was easy, because even when Mrs. Grote came out of her room, she hardly looked at her. It was as if she wanted to pretend Dorothy wasn't there.

Mr. Grote spent his days outside—hunting and fishing, bringing back squirrels and wild turkeys, whiskery fish, now and then a white-tailed deer. "I built this house with my own two hands," he told Dorothy the first night. "And we get along just fine. I don't have to work for nobody else." A few chickens and an old goat lived in the backyard, and with eggs and goat's milk and fish and possum, he told her, he could feed his family.

The day after she arrived, Mr. Grote showed Dorothy how to skin the squirrels he killed to make a stew he called gallimaufry, adding onions and vegetables, mustard, ginger, and vinegar. Though looking at those skinned squirrels turned her stomach, before long Dorothy was hungry enough to eat it. Then she would herd the little children into bed, trying to wash them first, but they cried and squirmed away. Mabel's hair looked as if it hadn't been washed in weeks. Dorothy couldn't get a comb through it, and the little girl screamed when she tried.

Dorothy felt as if *she'd* been thrown overboard without a life raft. How could she possibly stay afloat?

Chapter Twelve

Molly jumps off the Island Explorer bus, feeling satisfied. Vivian let her get rid of a whole box full of musty paperbacks and then answered questions for her project while they sipped tea in the living room. Molly's head is full of names—Maisie and Mam, Fanny and Dutchy, Mrs. Bryne, Mr. Grote. And the little recorder in her backpack is full of stories.

Gray clouds are crowding out the last bit of glowing blue in the evening sky, and a damp, chilly wind feels more like winter than spring. It works its way under the collar of Molly's jacket and makes her shiver as she walks toward Ralph and Dina's.

It feels good to open the door and enter the warm kitchen. Even though Molly doesn't eat meat anymore, her mouth starts to water at the smell of the bacon Dina's fried to crumble into the macaroni and cheese.

Ralph and Dina, sitting at the table, both turn their

faces to Molly. Their plates, she sees, are mostly clean.

"What happened to you?" Dina demands.

"I was at Vivian's." Molly hesitates, her backpack over her shoulder. Dina's voice says she's in trouble. Ralph's looking at his plate, smearing cheesy sauce around with his fork.

"Well, you can tell *Vivian* that you're supposed to get home by dinnertime," Dina says, standing up and pushing her chair back. "And you can remember that too."

"I guess I lost track of time." Molly doesn't move to take off her backpack or jacket. She doesn't want food now anyway. Her stomach is clenched tight, her appetite gone.

"You've got a phone, don't you? That we got for you? With the time on it?" Dina thumps her dishes into the sink.

"Yes. I just..." There aren't any words, right? Nothing she can say to make Dina stop being mad. "I'm sorry."

Molly looks from Dina's face, to the cheesy pasta with bacon on top, to Ralph, who still hasn't looked up.

"I wasn't that hungry anyway," she says, and walks through the kitchen to her room.

She closes the door, careful not to slam it—that would just give Dina something else to get on her case about. She dumps her backpack and jacket on the bed, pulls out the recorder and her social studies notebook, and sits at her desk. Her fingers are shaking a little. She makes a fist and tightens her muscles, then relaxes. Now her hand is steady.

What does she care if Dina's mad? If she doesn't get dinner? It's not like skipping one meal is the worst thing that ever happened to her. Molly pulls out a pen and presses the button on the recorder, ready to write down all that Vivian has told her.

Her stomach growls. She ignores it.

DOROTHY
HEMINGFORD COUNTY, MINNESOTA, 1930

On Monday morning, three days after she'd arrived, Mr. Grote shook Dorothy's shoulder in the dark room. It was time to get ready for school.

At some point in the night one of the younger children ended up snuggled against Dorothy's back, and Mabel had her head tucked into the crook of her arm. Dorothy wiggled out of the warm nest under the blankets, leaving the younger children sleeping. Spring or not, the room was so cold she could see her breath.

She put on one of her new dresses with both sweaters

on top, stockings, sturdy black shoes, and Fanny's mittens.

Then she ran to the pump outside and filled a pitcher with cold water, bringing it inside to heat on the stove. After she poured the warm water into a bowl, she took a rag and scrubbed her face, her neck, her fingernails. She used her fingers as a comb and divided her unwashed hair into pigtails and braided them as tightly as she could. She was as clean as she could manage without taking a bath. And how could she take a bath, in this place?

The other children crawled and stumbled out of the bedroom as she was gulping down the little breakfast she could find—wild rice pudding made with goat's milk and maple syrup boiled down from sap. The thought of getting out of the dark, smelly, crowded cabin for the day made her scoop up little Harold and swing him around. He crowed with surprised laughter. Dorothy knew it was risky—she might wake Mrs. Grote—but it was the happiest sound she'd heard yet in this place. She shared her rice pudding with Mabel, who blinked and looked her solemnly in the eye for the first time, then swallowed a spoonful eagerly.

Mr. Grote drew a map for her with a knife in the dirt—she would have to go down the drive, turn left, walk till she got to a T section, then go over a bridge till she reached the county road. Half an hour, give or take. A man named Mr. Post would be waiting for her in his truck at the main road at 8:30.

Dorothy slipped two eggs she had boiled the night before into the pocket of her mustard-colored coat and set off down the driveway. The fresh air, even though it made her nose feel numb and her cheeks tingle, was lovely in her throat. She couldn't keep her feet from skipping on the path.

For the next several hours, she would be free of the Grotes, free of the cramped and cavelike house, free of the demands of the children, who needed more than she could ever give them, free of Mrs. Grote's mood, which hung over the house like a heavy fog.

Once on the main road, Dorothy heard the truck before she could see it. It stopped with a great screeching of brakes, and an apple-faced man in a tan cap peered out at her. "Come on, darlin'. Don't have all day," he called.

She climbed into the back, where two planks made benches to sit on. There was a heap of horse blankets in a corner. Four kids were already on the benches, blankets around their shoulders. Dorothy got one for herself and sat on a bench, gripping it with her mittened hands whenever they hit a bump.

The truck made two more stops, and soon eight

kids were crammed into the back. They climbed a steep driveway before grinding to a stop. The children jumped out and formed a line. Dorothy took her place at the end, following the others to a small white clapboard schoolhouse with a bell in front.

A young woman in a cornflower blue dress, with a lavender scarf around her neck, was standing at the front door. Her face was pretty and lively, with big brown eyes and a wide smile. Her shiny brown hair was pulled back with a white ribbon.

"Welcome, children. Proceed in orderly fashion, as always." Her voice was high and clear. "Good morning, Michael . . . Bertha . . . Darlene," she said. When Dorothy reached her, she smiled. "Now—I haven't met you yet, but I heard you were coming. I'm Miss Larsen. And you must be—"

"Niamh," the girl said, just as Miss Larsen said "Dorothy."

Miss Larsen looked surprised. "Did I get that wrong? Or do you have a nickname?"

Dorothy felt her cheeks redden. "No, ma'am. It's just . . . my name used to be Niamh. Sometimes I forget about Dorothy. Nobody really calls me anything at my new house."

"Well." Miss Larsen's eyes rested on the girl's face. "I can call you Niamh, if you like."

"It's all right." She didn't want to draw any more attention to herself than she'd already done. "Dorothy is fine."

"As you wish. Lucy?" The teacher turned to another girl. "Would you mind showing Dorothy to her desk?"

Dorothy followed Lucy into a closet lined with hooks, where they hung up their coats before entering a large, sunny room. Dorothy felt her heart easing inside her chest.

The room was cozy and warm from the woodstove in the corner. Large windows let in the sun. Dorothy saw a desk for the teacher, rows of benches and work spaces, and slate blackboards along two walls, with posters of the alphabet and multiplication tables above. And books! Low shelves were filled with rows and rows of books.

Dorothy took a deep breath, inhaling the smell of clean wood and fresh paper and chalk. She could almost smell the sunshine. If she got to come here every day, she thought, maybe she could survive living with the Grotes after all.

There were twenty-three students, Dorothy learned. The youngest was six, the oldest sixteen. They were from farms and homes deep in the woods, and Dorothy wasn't, as she'd feared, behind everyone else. Even some of the older ones were just learning to read.

When Miss Larsen talked to Dorothy, she bent down and looked her in the eye. When she asked questions, she waited patiently for an answer. She smelled of lemons and vanilla. And after she'd given Dorothy a test to see how well she could read, she handed her a hardcover book with a green cloth cover.

"*Anne of Green Gables*," Miss Larsen said. "I think you will enjoy it, Dorothy."

At recess, Lucy invited Dorothy to play games with the other girls. Annie Annie Over. Pump, Pump, Pull Away. Ring Around the Rosie.

When Dorothy got out of the truck at 4:30 to head up the long road back to the Grotes' cabin, her steps were slow.

MOLLY
SPRUCE HARBOR, MAINE, PRESENT DAY

"I don't know," Tyler says one day, in social studies. They've just watched a film about the Wabanakis. "I mean it happens all the time, all over the world, right? One group wins, another loses."

Mr. Reed raises his eyebrows. "Well, it's true that humans have been oppressing each other since time began," he says. "Do you think the oppressed groups should just accept it, then? Stop complaining?"

"Yeah," Tyler says. "I kind of feel like saying, 'Deal with it.'"

Hot anger surges up inside of Molly.

She's always known she was Native American, but during this class she's learned more. Learned about how, for more than four hundred years, the Wabanakis were lied to. How they made treaties that were broken, and had their land taken away from them. Couldn't get jobs, couldn't buy homes. And on top of all that, people treated them like it was their own fault. They called them dirty, redskins, savages. And now Tyler says, "Just deal with it?"

Before she can think about it, her hand goes up.

Mr. Reed looks at her with surprise. "Yes?"

"I'm part Wabanaki," she says.

Heads turn.

"Penobscot," she goes on. "And I just want to say that what happened to the Native Americans wasn't a fair fight. You can't take everything away from someone, everything they own and care about, and then just say, 'Deal with it.' That's not okay."

Tyler rolls his eyes.

Megan McDonald, one seat ahead of Molly, raises her hand. "If someone steals your phone or your laptop, the police don't just say, 'Deal with it,'" she says, shooting Tyler a dirty look. "So why is it different if somebody takes your land?"

"They just want to be treated fairly," someone in the back says.

Other people chime in, and Megan turns around in her seat to look at Molly.

"Penobscot, huh?" she whispers. "That's cool. Like Molly Molasses, right?"

Chapter Thirteen

MOLLY
SPRUCE HARBOR, MAINE, PRESENT DAY

Working in the attic with Vivian after school helps Molly wipe the memory of Tyler and his obnoxious comments out of her mind. Vivian doesn't want to throw out much, but Molly does organize three boxes, sorting everything inside, taping the boxes back up, writing down their contents in her notebook.

Vivian says she is too tired for any questions "with that odd little machine of yours," so Molly walks outside, drawing in deep breaths of fresh air to get the smell of dust out of her nose. Maybe it's for the best, anyway. She'd better get home before dinnertime today, or she'll have to deal with Dina again.

To her surprise, Jack is working in the yard with a rake. She wanders over. He's dragging dead leaves and grass off the flower beds, piling them up in heaps.

"Hey," Molly says. "I didn't know you'd be here."

"Vivian asked Mom if I could come and clean up the

yard a little. She's paying me," he says.

"So we're doing the same thing," Molly says with a grin. "Straightening up. Making things neater."

"Well, yeah," Jack says. "Except I'm actually working."

"What?" Molly stares at him, her smile vanishing.

Jack looks down at the leaves he's raked into a pile. "Mom says—it's just, she says you're not doing much. Up in the attic. Not throwing anything away."

Molly's mouth opens and closes. "That's not true. We're going through all the boxes. Organizing things, getting them all labeled. So they'll be easy to find."

Jack snorts. "Easy for who to find?"

Molly doesn't have an answer for that.

Jack drops the rake and turns to look at her. "See, you have to think about it from my mom's point of view. If you're not doing anything up in the attic, you're just wasting Vivian's time and tiring her out, and she's already an old lady—my mom's worried about that."

For the second time today, anger rises in Molly's chest. "Your mom," she says bitterly. Terry's always been suspicious of Molly. Just like Dina. Never willing to give her a chance, acting like Molly *wants* to be a foster kid. "She can't wait for me to get in trouble again, can she?"

Now Jack looks angry too. He snatches up the rake

and gets back to work. "Are you kidding?" he says, jabbing at the dead leaves. "My mom got you this job, remember? She lied to Vivian. She didn't tell her about you and that stupid book you stole. What if Vivian finds out? My mom could get fired. Did you ever think of that?"

He rakes hard, pulling the leaves toward him, ignoring Molly. Her heart sinks. Would Vivian really fire Terry because of her? She stares at Jack, but he refuses to look at her. Forget him, then. Forget Terry too. She stuffs her hands into the pockets of her jacket and walks away without another word.

DOROTHY
HEMINGFORD COUNTY, MINNESOTA, 1930

One day in late April, Miss Larsen sent Dorothy out to get firewood, and when she came back, the entire class was singing "Happy Birthday." To her!

"How did you know?" Dorothy asked Miss Larsen.

"It was in your paperwork," she answered.

Tears sprang to Dorothy's eyes. She couldn't remember the last time anyone had sung to her.

When she came home with a piece of birthday cake, Mr. Grote snorted, "How ridiculous, celebrating a birth date. I don't even know the day I was born. But let's have that cake."

The next few weeks were cold and gray. It even snowed a little in the nights. The bedcovers were thin, and the Grote children pulled them away from Dorothy in their sleep. She felt as if she'd never get warm. Lying awake, shivering in the darkness, she thought of the trip from Ireland, all the days on the ship. Those had seemed endless too. Once, her da had tried to help the time pass by telling all the kids to shut their eyes and imagine a perfect day.

Dorothy had imagined a Sunday afternoon, visiting her gram in her snug house on the edge of town. Climbing over stone walls, crossing a field of wild grass that moved like the waves on the sea. Gram's house in the distance with its thatched roof and whitewashed walls, pots of red geraniums blooming on the windowsill.

Inside, a goose roasted in the oven. The black-and-white dog, Monty, waited under the table for scraps. Gram rolled dough for a rhubarb tart and Dorothy sat on a stool until it was finished. Then the two of them went to sit in the front room, "the good room," Gram called it, for afternoon tea, strong and with plenty of sugar, and currant bread, sliced and warm.

Now, as she thought about the perfect day, she realized she'd never visit Gram again, never sip hot tea and eat fresh currant bread with her. Indeed, Dorothy was beginning to wonder if she'd ever eat a full meal again. Mr. Grote had returned from the woods empty-handed for the last three days, so there was hardly any food in the house. All they had to eat were some eggs from the chickens and old potatoes from the garden, and they were running low on both. It was getting hard for Dorothy to find anything to slip into her pocket to take to school for lunch.

On the evening of the third day, Dorothy could feel Mr. Grote looking at her as she sat on the floor with Harold, trying to show him the letters of his name. She'd brought an old board inside to write on and burned a stick in the fire to get charcoal to make black marks.

"What's that thing around your neck?" Mr. Grote asked.

Dorothy's hand flew up to her Claddagh cross. She knew why he was asking. "It's not worth anything."

"Looks like silver," Mr. Grote said. "Tarnished."

"It's tin," she lied.

"Lemme see." Mr. Grote came closer and touched the cross with its clasped hands, the crowned heart. "Who gave it to you?"

"My gram."

He frowned, peering at it. "Sure is strange-looking.

Those funny symbols. Don't think I could sell it if I tried."

Mrs. Grote had gotten out of bed for once and was slumped on the couch, the baby by her side. She watched them with a strange, sharp look from across the room.

Harold was squirming in Dorothy's lap, scratching his hair. She looked, pushed the boy's hand away, and looked again. The skin behind his ears was red and sore. She'd seen this before, on her twin brothers, on the boat coming over. Mam had been terrified of the kids getting lice and checked them all, day after day. "Worst thing in the world to get rid of," she'd said. But crowded together with strangers on that boat, there had been no way to prevent it.

Dorothy parted the strands of hair at Harold's neck and jerked her hand back. His hair was dark, so the tiny white nits showed up clearly, and she even saw something scuttle along his scalp. Though she knew it wasn't his fault, she had to stifle a sudden urge to dump the boy off her lap.

Mr. Grote was frowning at her. "What?"

She nodded at Harold's head. "Lice. They've probably all got it." She wanted to cry, knowing what would happen next. No more school for days. Everyone's hair chopped short—or off. Everything in this house would have to be cleaned with lye soap and drenched with boiling water—the bedsheets, the mattresses.

Mr. Grote groaned. He looked at Harold and made a face. Mrs. Grote stirred on the couch, looking hard at Dorothy.

"You brung the parasite into this house," she said.

Dorothy felt her face flame up. "No, ma'am. I did not."

"They came from somewhere," Mrs. Grote said, still staring hard.

Dorothy thought of Mrs. Grote's bed, where she spent most of her time. The sheets were almost never washed. Dorothy had aired out the blankets and quilts on the children's beds a few times. But whenever she had gone into Mrs. Grote's room, she'd been ordered out at once.

"I think . . ." she said, working up her courage. "I think you might need to check your bed. And your hair." She couldn't stop looking at Mrs. Grote's long hair, dull and matted.

For the first time since Dorothy had been in her house, Mrs. Grote sat bolt upright. She pushed Nettie aside. "You brung it," she said. "I told Gerald it was too much, having a vagrant in this house when Lord knows where she's been. Irish bogtrotter. I told you!"

"Wilma," her husband said. "Quiet down."

"I won't!" Mrs. Grote got to her feet, more quickly

than Dorothy had ever seen her move. "She comes in here, acting all high and mighty, like she's better than us. I didn't want her. It was you! And now see what she's done. Bringing filthy bugs in here. We have to get rid of her!"

Mr. Grote stood, looking back and forth between Dorothy and his wife. "Easy, Wilma. Calm down."

"I want that girl—that filth—out of my house."

"Let's talk about this."

"I want her out!"

"All right, all right." He looked at Dorothy with dull eyes, and she could see him giving up. He wasn't going to fight with his wife, not about her.

Mrs. Grote disappeared down the hall and returned a moment later with Dorothy's suitcase. She heaved it across the room. It crashed against the wall, spilling its contents across the floor. But when Dorothy made a move to grab what she could get, Mrs. Grote tried to stomp on her fingers. Dorothy flinched back.

Her boots and the mustard-colored coat, with Fanny's precious warm mittens in the pocket, were on a nail by the front door. Dorothy snatched up both and stumbled out onto the porch, shivering, her breath coming out in puffs of white. She was wearing the blue chambray dress she'd made at the Byrnes, her white sweater, the only pair of stockings she owned that weren't all holes, and the cross around her neck.

As she struggled to pull her boots on with trembling fingers, Dorothy heard Mr. Grote say, "What if something happens to her?"

"If that stupid girl gets it into her head to run away, there's nothing we can do, is there?" his wife snapped.

And run Dorothy did. She hurried down the steps of the porch, buttoning up the coat as she went. She could feel the sewing packet Fanny made for her in the garment's inner pocket. But everything else she had to leave behind: her brown suitcase, the other dresses she'd made at the Byrnes', her change of underwear, the navy sweater, her schoolbooks and pencil . . . and four young children she was powerless to help. They would have to learn to make it on their own.

Chapter Fourteen

Molly decides it's time for her to start making her own lunch. Peanut butter and honey. That way Dina can't sigh and look irritated about the extra work, and Molly will end up with something she can actually eat.

The question is, where is she going to eat it?

Everyone in the school cafeteria has their own territory. The jocks take over the back section, near the wall. The band kids sit at a table to Molly's left, with most of the theater kids nearby. Usually Molly sits at the second table from the door with Jack and some of his soccer buddies.

Molly hesitates for a moment in the door to the lunchroom. No one is sitting at the second table from the door. If she sits there alone, it'll look like she's waiting for Jack.

She's tempted to turn and run. She could go to the

bathroom and avoid the lunchroom altogether. Or maybe she should go to the science lab where she and Lori sometimes sit. . . .

But why should she run? Just because Jack got the idea from his mom that Molly isn't doing her job—and chose to believe it—doesn't mean she should change *her* plans.

She's sitting at her usual table, taking the peanut-butter-and-honey sandwich out of her lunch bag, when Jack walks by. He doesn't even meet Molly's eye. No hi, no nod, no smile. For a second she wonders if he saw her—but of course he saw her. Then he's gone, heading for a table in the back. A few soccer players yell his name.

Molly stuffs nearly half of the sandwich in her mouth. She'll eat as quickly as possible, and then she's out of here. The bread is flimsy and tasteless; she must've spread the peanut butter too thick. She feels like she's about to choke.

"Hey, Molly? Is something wrong?"

Molly blinks and stares up at Megan, who's standing by the table looking at her with concern, her hair brushing the shoulders of her bright green T-shirt.

Molly shakes her head.

"Okay if I sit down?" Megan takes a seat across from

Molly. "You look upset. I thought maybe Tyler said something again. What a troglodyte, huh?"

Molly's still chewing. It seems to take years before she finally manages to swallow. "Yeah," she says a little breathlessly.

"I mean, it's the twenty-first century, you know? Guess he never got the memo."

Molly's not quite sure what Megan's doing here. Doesn't she have a table she usually sits at? Friends waiting for her? But Megan is unwrapping a sandwich—is that hummus, Molly wonders?—like it's no big deal.

Megan takes a little plastic tub of carrot sticks out of her lunch bag. "I kind of like social studies, actually. I'm a total dork like that." She laughs. "I even like the portaging project. It's cool learning about how people used to live. Not the stuff about battles and wars, though. I hate all that killing. I'm a vegetarian. Do you know what they do to chickens?"

"Yeah, I saw a video online," Molly says. "It's pretty bad. I don't eat meat either."

"I knew you were cool!" Megan beams. Her smile is so bright, even her freckles seem to light up. Hesitantly, Molly smiles back. A little bit of her hopes that Jack is paying attention.

Megan bites a carrot in half. "Who are you

interviewing? Your grandparents or somebody?"

Molly shakes her head. "Actually, this old lady I work for."

"You've got a job?"

Molly isn't about to explain exactly how she ended up cleaning Vivian's attic. "I'm just kind of helping her out. She's ninety or something."

Megan's eyes grow wide. "Aw, lucky! You must be getting great answers. Ninety! I'm interviewing my grandmother, and she's only sixty-two. I'm going to the library after school to do some research on the computer. Find some pictures to use with my report and stuff. You want to come?"

Molly digs in her lunch bag for the bunch of grapes she put there, giving herself time to think. The library? She can't go back to the library. What if Mrs. LeBlanc is there? What if she orders Molly, the book thief, to get out? What if she insists on searching Molly's backpack in front of everybody? In front of Megan?

"I can't today," she mumbles.

"Okay. Maybe another time?"

"I just—um. I can't." Molly stuffs her grapes back into her paper bag and gets up. "I have to go."

Megan looks confused. "Okay, well . . . bye."

"Bye." As she's leaving, Molly hears the entire table

of soccer players laughing, as if somebody's just made some hilarious joke.

DOROTHY
HEMINGFORD COUNTY, MINNESOTA, 1930

Trudging forward like a sleepwalker in the dark, Dorothy made her way down the driveway. Then she turned left and plodded up the rutted dirt road to the falling-down bridge. Gravel crunched loudly under her boots. Crystal stars glittered overhead, and a full moon glowed with a pearly light between the branches on the trees.

Where could she go? It was impossible to return to the Grotes. A part of her was relieved. That dreadful house, the needy children, the filth . . . was there lice in her own hair too? The thought made her head itch. She took off Fanny's mittens to scratch her head, then stuffed them back on, shoving her hands deep into the pockets of her coat.

But along with the relief came fear. Where was she going to go? What was she going to do?

There was something in her right pocket—she could feel it through the mitten. She fished it out.

Dutchy's penny.

"For luck," he'd said. Well, it hadn't worked. It was

hard to imagine two unluckier places than the Byrnes'
and the Grotes'.

"I know my fate, don't I?" Dutchy had told her.
"You're the one getting back on that train."

And now here she was again, on her way to some-
place new, without knowing who would take her in—if
anyone.

Dorothy tucked the coin back into her pocket. She'd
walk all the way to school, she decided. Four miles. At
least she'd have shelter for the night there.

She counted a hundred steps and started again. And
again. And again. After a while, she wanted to sink
down beside the road. Her feet were aching; her face
was numb. The sky was dark, and she was so tired. But
she didn't dare lie down. If she stopped moving, she
wouldn't get to the school. She might freeze.

Dorothy tried to think of nothing but counting
steps.

Finally, in the dim moonlight, after what seemed
like hours, she spied the white schoolhouse up ahead.
When she reached the building she tugged on the knob
of the front door with her mittened hands. It was locked.
She went around to the back, to the porch where they
kept the wood for the stove, and yanked on that door.
It opened easily and she fell on the floor.

There was another door to the schoolroom here, but

it, too, was locked. Dorothy found an old horse blanket, scratchy and smelly, folded on top of the woodpile, and wrapped it around herself, huddling against the logs for warmth. Despite the cold, she was exhausted enough to fall into a sound sleep.

"Dorothy?" She felt a hand shaking her shoulder. "What in the world . . . ?"

For a moment she wasn't sure where she was. She looked around at the pile of rough-cut wood and the wide whitewashed planks of the porch walls and blinked in the clear morning light. Then she looked up at the round red cheeks and puzzled expression of Mr. Post. He must have come in early to start a fire in the schoolhouse stove.

Mr. Post stared at Dorothy and shook his head. Then he helped her up and took her into the schoolroom, where he guided her to a chair and put her feet on another chair. He took the dirty horse blanket away and brought a clean plaid one from a closet to drape over her legs. He unlaced her boots and took them off, tsking at the holes in her stockings. When she was settled and comfortable, he gathered wood and kindling for the fire.

Dorothy just watched. She didn't have the energy to move; she didn't have a thought in her head. Slowly the warmth of the stove began to penetrate her skin. Then Miss Larsen arrived.

"What's this?" she asked. She unwrapped her lavender scarf and took off her hat and gloves. Kneeling beside Dorothy's chair, she said, "Goodness, child."

Mr. Post was putting on his hat and gloves. "She was asleep out there on the porch when I arrived," he said. "Scared the bejeezus out of me. Well, I'm off to get the others."

As soon as he left in the truck, Miss Larsen said, "Now then. Tell me what happened."

And Dorothy did. She had not been planning to tell more than she had to, but her teacher's friendly brown eyes were so sharp with concern that everything came tumbling out. Mrs. Grote lying in bed all day, Mr. Grote in the woods, the moldy old mattresses and holes in the floor, the children squalling with hunger. Dorothy told her about how Mrs. Grote had called her a filthy Irish bogtrotter. She told her about the long walk in the dark to the schoolhouse. "If I didn't have the mittens a kind woman—Fanny—made for me at the last place, I don't know what I would've done."

Miss Larsen put her hand over Dorothy's and left it there, squeezing every now and then. "Oh, my poor girl," she said.

And then, "Thank goodness for the mittens. Fanny

143

sounds like a good friend."

"She was."

Miss Larsen cocked her head. "Who brought you to the Grotes?"

"Mr. Sorenson from the Children's Aid Society."

"All right. When Mr. Post gets back, I'll send him out to find this Mr. Sorenson." Opening her lunch pail, she pulled out a biscuit. "You must be hungry."

Normally Dorothy would refuse. She knew this was Miss Larsen's lunch. But the hunger inside her was so fierce that she couldn't say no. She seized the biscuit and devoured it in three bites.

Miss Larsen heated water on the stove for tea and cut an apple into slices, arranging them on a chipped china plate from a shelf. She poured the tea into cups, added sugar, and brought them over. The worst of her hunger tamed now, Dorothy could pick up an apple slice in trembling fingers and eat it slowly. The sweetness made her eyes water.

"Miss Larsen," she said. "Could you ever—would you ever—"

Dorothy couldn't finish. It was too much to ask, she knew. But she couldn't help wanting it.

"Take you home to live with me?" Miss Larsen asked gently.

Dorothy nodded, a lump in her throat so large that

she couldn't swallow the bite of apple in her mouth. She looked away from her teacher, away from the sadness she could already see in her eyes.

"I care about you, Dorothy. I think you know that," Miss Larsen said. "But I can't—I'm in no position to take care of a girl. I live in a boardinghouse."

Dorothy nodded, not looking up.

"I will help you find a home," her teacher said. "A place that is safe and clean, where you'll be treated like a ten-year-old girl. I promise you that."

Maybe Dorothy should have been happy to hear Miss Larsen's promise. Somewhere safe and clean, somewhere she did not have to sew all day long, somewhere she'd be fed and warm. It should have sounded like heaven.

But even more than heaven, what she wanted right at that moment was for Miss Larsen to put her arms around her. To take her home to live with her. To love her like her own child.

But that wasn't what she was going to get. Dorothy put a shaky hand out to her teacup and gulped the hot tea, trying to melt the knot in her throat.

The other children came in, and Dorothy took her seat beside Lucy. Miss Larsen talked quietly to Mr. Post and he went out again. In a kind of daze Dorothy copied what Lucy did—getting out her spelling primer, opening to the right page, lining up behind her to write on the board.

Lucy squeezed her hand. "Are you all right?"

Dorothy nodded.

But it was a lie. She wasn't all right. She was still cold, still tired, still hungry. She didn't have a home to go to. And no matter what Miss Larsen had promised, she was afraid that maybe she never would.

Chapter Fifteen

MOLLY
SPRUCE HARBOR, MAINE, PRESENT DAY

In the kitchen at Ralph and Dina's on Saturday morning, Molly spoons up the last of her Raisin Bran. She rinses off the bowl and puts it in the dishwasher, careful to leave no extra work for Dina.

Looking out through the window, she spots Dina outside, raking one of the flower beds. Molly's surprised—she's never seen Dina in the garden. She wanders outside to see what she's doing.

Heaps of dead leaves are lying on the grass. In the newly bare earth, little green sprouts are poking up.

"What are those?" Molly asks.

"Crocuses," Dina answers, not looking up.

"Oh, yeah. My mom and I used to plant those every spring."

Did she actually say that? And to Dina, of all people? But the memory rose up so suddenly and vividly that the words just popped out. Every Easter when Molly was little, she went to St. Anne's Church with her parents. There was a big table in front of the sanctuary, covered with crocuses in little pots wrapped in silver foil. Molly would pick the one she liked best, and she and her mom would plant it in the cold mud beside the driveway. A cluster of crocuses bloomed there every spring, white and purple and gold.

"How about you help me, then? You like cleaning up." Dina pushes the rake at Molly. "Why don't you go get the leaves off that other bed?"

Molly hesitates. "I've never raked before."

"No big trick to it." Dina lets go of the rake, so Molly has to grab it. "Just pull the leaves off. You need to let the sunlight touch the earth."

Dina heads to the garage. Molly walks slowly over to the other flower bed and tentatively uses the rake to pull a clump of soggy brown leaves onto the grass.

Molly thinks of Mary Lennox and her friend Dickon, shut inside the walled and secret garden, weeding and digging, giving the neglected flowers a chance to flourish. She likes the idea that she's doing the same thing. Okay, it's just Ralph and Dina's yard, which is small and only has two flower beds and some discouraged-looking yew bushes. It's not exactly the formal garden of Misselthwaite Manor. But still.

She rakes harder, thinking about the book.

Dina comes out of the garage, trundling a wheelbarrow in front of her. "What are you doing?" Dina is suddenly next to her, grabbing the rake out of her hand.

Molly blinks at her. "Raking. Like you said."

"You have to be gentle."

Molly looks down at the rake to see several shreds of green tangled among its teeth. She's pulled a crocus up by the roots.

"Oh. Sorry," she mumbles.

Dina sighs. "It's all right. I'll do it myself."

DOROTHY
HEMINGFORD COUNTY, MINNESOTA, 1930

Later in the afternoon, while all the children were copying math from the board, a dark green Chrysler pulled up into the schoolyard behind Mr. Post's truck. Out the window, Dorothy could see Mr. Sorenson walking toward the schoolhouse, taking off his black felt hat.

Miss Larsen greeted him at the door and spoke quietly for a moment. Then she turned back to the students and clapped her hands. "All right, everyone! Let's take a break. It's a beautiful day—you can have ten minutes outside. Dorothy, you stay in here with me." She led Mr. Sorenson to a chair near the stove and asked

Dorothy to explain to him exactly what had happened.

Dorothy twisted her fingers together and looked down at them. Telling Miss Larsen had been one thing—she'd been sure her teacher would understand. Mr. Sorenson, though . . .

Miss Larsen nodded at Dorothy. "Start with last night," she suggested gently.

"I was looking after Harold," Dorothy began. "He had . . . I'm afraid there were . . . lice in his hair." She glanced up quickly enough to see an expression of distaste cross Mr. Sorenson's face. He looked like he wanted to inch his chair away from her. "And Mrs. Grote said . . . she said I'd brought them into the house. She called me . . ." She didn't want to repeat the words.

"My, my," Mr. Sorenson said when Dorothy had finished her story. He stroked his mustache. "Such a long walk in the cold. You must have been very . . ." His voice trailed off. "And yet. And yet. I wonder."

Dorothy's heart started to beat more quickly.

He looked at Miss Larsen. "A ten-year-old girl. Don't you find, Miss Larsen, that there can be a certain—excitability? A tendency to exaggerate, perhaps?"

"It depends on the girl, Mr. Sorenson," she said stiffly, lifting her chin. "I have never known Dorothy to lie."

Chuckling, he shook his head. "Ah, Miss Larsen,

that's not at all what I meant. I merely meant that some-times, children—well, they take things very much to heart. And in a few days, all's well again. Now, I'm sure there was a disagreement. Voices raised, perhaps. It does happen. And of course I saw with my own eyes that the Grotes' household. . . . Well, it is not, perhaps, an ideal situation. But very few of us have perfect fami-lies, do we? And when we are dependent on the charity of others, we are not always in a position to complain." He smiled at Dorothy. "I think you should go back. Give it another try."

"She told me to get out," Dorothy whispered slowly, the words like icy pebbles on her tongue.

Miss Larsen's eyes were glittering, and a red flush had crept up her neck. "Did you hear the girl, Mr. Sorenson?" she asked. "Surely you don't expect Doro-thy to return to that situation. Frankly, I wonder why you don't ask the police to go out there and take a look. It doesn't sound like a healthy place for the other chil-dren, either."

Mr. Sorenson was nodding slowly. "Well, then, you see . . . if Dorothy isn't willing to return . . . we're in a bit of a pickle. There are no families that I know of at the moment seeking orphans. I could inquire, of course. Contact the Children's Aid in New York. If it comes down to it, Dorothy could go back there, I suppose, on the next train that comes through."

"Surely we won't need to resort to that," Miss Larsen said.

He gave a little shrug. "One would hope not. One doesn't know."

Miss Larsen put her hand on Dorothy's shoulder and gave it a squeeze. "Let's explore our options, then, Mr. Sorenson, shall we? And in the meantime—for a day or two—Dorothy can come home with me."

Dorothy looked up at her with surprise. "But I thought—"

"It can't be permanent," she said quickly. "I live in a boardinghouse, Mr. Sorenson, where no children are allowed. But my landlady has a kind heart, and I think she will be sympathetic. As I said—for a day or two."

Mr. Sorenson stroked his mustache again. "Very well, Miss Larsen. I will look into other possibilities and leave you in charge of Dorothy for a few days. Young lady, I trust that you will be polite and well behaved."

"Yes, sir," Dorothy said solemnly, trying to hide the fact that her heart was beating hard again, leaping with joy.

Chapter Sixteen

MOLLY
SPRUCE HARBOR, MAINE, PRESENT DAY

In Vivian's attic, Molly tugs the lid off a white cardboard box. Inside, all she can see is masses of tissue paper. She grabs a bunch of it, feels something heavy inside. The paper has been wrapped many times around whatever is in the middle.

"Take care with that!" Vivian says anxiously.

"I *am* taking care!"

She makes her hands go slowly, unwinding what feels like miles and miles of soft, thin paper. Once she gets to the center, she finds a teacup, thin and fragile. Red roses bloom across the glossy surface of the china.

"It's not broken, is it?" Vivian asks, coming to hover over Molly's shoulder.

"You think I broke it?"

Vivian looks down at her in surprise. "Gracious, child, you're in a mood today. What's wrong?"

"Nothing. I just—I don't break stuff." Molly sets the

teacup carefully down on the attic floor and picks up another wad of paper from the box. Now she goes even more slowly, unwrapping the paper an inch at a time to find a little milk pitcher.

"I know that. You don't think I've noticed that about you?" Vivian returns to her seat on an old chest.

"Some people haven't," Molly mutters.

"Which people are those?"

Molly unwraps another bundle. A sugar bowl. She sets it on the floor. "Dina," she says, concentrating on her hands.

"Your foster mother?"

Molly makes a face. "She's not any kind of mother to me."

"Well, I won't call her that, then. The woman you're staying with?"

"I can't do anything right!" Molly bursts out. "She's mad at me about *everything*. No matter what I do, it's not good enough."

Molly waits for Vivian to tell her that she just has to try harder, be more polite, be a better kid. And Dina will magically turn into the perfect foster mom. Because that's the sort of thing adults always say about other adults.

But Vivian doesn't say anything like that. For a few moments she's silent. Then she says, "Life throws us

154

together with all sorts of people. And we don't have much choice about most of them. Certainly not when we're young."

Molly glances over at her. This isn't what she expected to hear.

"People don't always give us what we need," Vivian continues, looking steadily at the tea set. "Sometimes they just won't. But often it's because they simply can't."

Molly isn't ready to feel sympathy for Dina—not yet. But at least Vivian isn't telling her that she'll magically come to like her, if she gives her a chance. Molly unwraps and unwraps. A teapot. Two more cups. Soon the entire tea set is on the dusty attic floorboards.

"Nothing's broken?" Vivian asks.

"Not a single chip in the whole set," Molly confirms.

A broad smile crosses Vivian's face. "Now that is a lovely surprise. I never would have expected such a fragile thing to last so long."

DOROTHY
HEMINGFORD COUNTY, MINNESOTA, 1930

Miss Larsen's boardinghouse was tall and narrow, light blue, with carved white trim around the roofline and the front porch. After the Grotes', it seemed like something from another world to Dorothy. She felt she should step on the wood floors gently so they didn't creak, keep her hands to her sides in case they smudged the burgundy wallpaper in the hallway.

"Wait here," Miss Larsen whispered, touching a finger to her lips. She pulled off her gloves, unwrapped the scarf from around her neck, and disappeared through a door.

Dorothy perched anxiously on the edge of a horsehair armchair, ready to jump up again if someone arrived.

After a few minutes, Miss Larsen came back. "My landlady, Mrs. Murphy, would like to meet you," she said. "I told her about your—predicament. I hope that's all right. I felt she needed to understand why I brought you here."

Dorothy nodded.

"Just be yourself, Dorothy," she said. "All right, then. This way."

Dorothy followed her down the hall and through the door into a parlor. A plump woman with a fluff of downy gray hair around her face was sitting on a rose-colored velvet sofa. "Well, my girl, it sounds as if you've had quite a time of it," she said, waving her hand for Dorothy to sit in one of the many chairs.

"Yes, ma'am." Dorothy glanced at Miss Larsen, who smiled and motioned toward the chair beside her.

As Dorothy took a seat, Mrs. Murphy said, "Oh—you're Irish, are you?"

Her heart sank a little, thinking of Mrs. Grote's words. "Yes, ma'am," she murmured.

Mrs. Murphy beamed. "I thought so! Well, and I'm Irish too. Came over like you as a wee lass. My people are from Enniscorthy. And yours?"

Dorothy's heart bounded back up again. "Kinvara. In County Galway."

"Indeed, I know the place! My cousin married a Kinvara girl. And you were christened Dorothy?"

"No, Niamh. My name was changed by the first family I came to." Dorothy felt afraid the minute the words were out of her mouth. She'd just confessed to being thrown out of two homes.

But Mrs. Murphy didn't seem worried. "I guessed as much! Dorothy is no Irish name." Dorothy relaxed, just a little. Mrs. Murphy seemed to like her, or at least to like that she was from Ireland. So surely she would agree to what Miss Larsen asked and let her stay. For a day or two at least. And maybe—Dorothy dared to hope—even longer.

Mrs. Murphy poured them both tea in cups painted with roses. Dorothy sipped hers cautiously, dreading what might happen if she spilled, or worse, dropped this beautiful piece of china. But nothing dreadful happened, and after the tea was drunk, Miss Larsen took her up to her room, a tidy, bright little space barely big enough for a single bed, a tall oak dresser, and a narrow pine desk with a brass lamp. There were watercolor pictures of flowers hanging on the walls and lace curtains on the window.

On the dresser was a photograph in a frame of a bearded man in a dark suit, standing stiffly behind a slim woman seated in a straight-backed chair. The woman, in a black dress, looked stern, but her bright brown eyes were familiar.

"Are these your parents?" Dorothy asked shyly.

"Yes." Miss Larsen came close and gazed at the picture. "They're both dead now, so I suppose that makes me an orphan too."

Dinner, which Dorothy and Miss Larsen ate with Mrs. Murphy and the other four boarders, was at six o'clock. There was a bounty of food: a ham in the middle of the table, roasted potatoes, Brussels sprouts glistening with butter, a basket of rolls. Dorothy felt the pressure of tears in her eyes. She made herself eat slowly, savoring the saltiness of the ham, the softness of the rolls, the buttery crunch of the vegetables. After dinner Mrs. Murphy showed Dorothy to a room of her own, with crisp white sheets on the bed, a pillow, and two clean quilts. Dorothy put out a shy finger to stroke the top quilt, touching the patches of blue and purple cotton. The little room was so clean and warm that Dorothy felt dizzy, as if she were floating.

Mrs. Murphy handed her a nightgown, underclothes, a towel and hand cloth, and a brush for her teeth. "The bathroom is down the hall," she said. "Go and run yourself a bath."

Dorothy dropped her eyes to the rug. She knew she had to say something, but it was almost impossible.

"Gracious, child. Don't look so alarmed. What is it?"

"I'm afraid . . ." Dorothy whispered with shame. "Maybe . . . there are nits in my hair."

"Oh." Understanding filled the landlady's face. "Well, it's to be expected, isn't it? Living in that dreadful place. Are you sure?"

Dorothy shook her head.

"It's good to check, of course."

"I'm sorry."

"It's not your fault, child! Just wait here." Mrs. Murphy bustled away, and a minute or two later, Miss Larsen came in with a comb and a determinedly bright look on her face. Dorothy sat on the edge of the bed and bowed her head while Miss Larsen tugged the comb through her hair. The girl gritted her teeth as the comb's teeth pulled through tangles and scraped across her scalp. After several tense minutes, Miss Larsen sighed.

"Dorothy, I think you have nothing to worry about. Thank goodness. I'll tell Mrs. Murphy. You take as long as you like in the bath. Mrs. Murphy says that the others can use a different powder room tonight."

Tears of relief stinging her eyes, Dorothy clutched her towel and walked slowly down the hallway to the bathroom.

Once there, she looked in the mirror. It was the first time since she'd arrived in Minnesota that she'd had a chance to gaze carefully at her own reflection.

A girl she barely recognized looked back. Thin and pale, with sharp cheekbones and matted red hair. Her cheeks and nose sore and chapped. Scabbed lips. Her sweater covered with an oily layer of dirt.

Dorothy swallowed. Her throat hurt, and there was a dull ache in her chest as well. Maybe she was getting sick. She turned away from the mirror and ran the water in the bath. Once she'd scrubbed all the dirt off and rubbed soap furiously through her hair, she let the water drain out, then filled the tub again. She lay back in the warm water and closed her eyes. After a long time, she finally pulled herself out of the bath. She was so tired it was almost impossible to dry herself with the towel, pull on her nightclothes, and crawl into bed.

And there's where she stayed for her first week at Mrs. Murphy's house.

Dorothy slept and slept and slept, with the covers pulled up and the shades drawn. At some point a doctor came, put his cold metal stethoscope to her chest, and announced that she had pneumonia.

Mrs. Murphy set a little bell by her bed and told her to shake it if she needed anything while Miss Larsen was away at school. "I'm just downstairs," she said. She placed a pitcher of water and a glass by her bed and brought Dorothy bowls of warm chicken soup filled with carrots and celery and potatoes.

When Dorothy at last felt strong enough to leave her bed, she found she had no clothes to put on. Mrs. Murphy had taken away the blue dress and the white sweater she'd been wearing when she arrived. "Not even fit for the ragbag," she said briskly when she got to Dorothy's room and found her sitting on the edge of the bed in her nightgown. "You come with me, girl. Let's see what we can do."

Mrs. Murphy led Dorothy, still barefoot, out into the hallway. Against one wall was a wooden trunk, which Mrs. Murphy pulled open. They both knelt down to peer inside.

"My boarders don't always take everything with them when they move on," Mrs. Murphy explained, lifting folded garments out of the trunk. "Sometimes they don't have space to pack everything, or something's unfashionable, or they don't care for it as much as they once did. But I keep it all. You never know what might be useful. Here, now." She held up a brown dress with pearl buttons. "A bit big, I'm sure. But you know how to use your needle, don't you?"

Dorothy nodded.

"Take it in a little and turn up the hem, and it'll do," Mrs. Murphy went on briskly. "And this will look quite lovely with that hair of yours!" A sky-blue cardigan embroidered with flowers landed on Dorothy's lap. She'd never seen anything so pretty. There were stockings, too, and even a pair of black shoes. Mrs. Murphy seemed pleased. "You'll look quite respectable in all that, I've no doubt. Go put it on, child."

Dorothy's fingers shook as she did up the buttons on the dress and slipped on the sweater. The new clothes smelled of cedar, to keep out the moths, and she told herself it was the smell that made her eyes water.

But with her health and her new clothes came a new worry—this surely wouldn't last. Didn't Miss Larsen say she could only stay for a few days? It had been more than a week. But she could not bear the thought of leaving.

Mrs. Murphy really seemed to like her. Maybe—just maybe—she had changed her mind.

Chapter Seventeen

MOLLY
SPRUCE HARBOR, MAINE, PRESENT DAY

On Sunday it rains. All day. Dina's annoyed because she can't finish the yard work. Ralph has retreated to the garage and is tinkering with the car. Molly lies on her bed, looking at the ceiling, *Anne of Green Gables* facedown on the quilt beside her.

She's been in Avonlea all morning. Anne has dyed her red hair green (even worse than a blue stripe, Molly thinks), accidentally gotten her best friend drunk, and nearly drowned pretending to be the Lady of Shalott. Molly thinks Dina has it easy, really, with an almost-orphan like her. She could have ended up with someone like Anne.

But Molly is tired of reading now. And what else can she do?

Her homework is done.

It's not her regular day to go over to Vivian's, and she can't just show up there. Terry would probably have her arrested for trespassing.

She can't straighten up her room anymore. It's as neat as it can get.

She certainly can't call Jack.

If only there was somebody else she could call. Megan? But Molly doesn't have her phone number. And even if she did, Megan probably thinks she's a freak, after the way Molly ran out of the lunchroom when Megan asked her to go to the library.

The library . . .

Molly wishes she *could* go to the library. It was a good idea Megan had, to look for pictures to go with her portaging project. What if Molly could find photos of the place in New York where Vivian lived, or the ship her family took from Ireland? Or the trains that all those orphans rode on? It would be cool for her report, and maybe she could even show Vivian.

But she can't do it. She's not welcome there.

Molly gets up and wanders over to her dresser. She brushes her hair and examines the fading blue stripe. She looks down at her necklace with its three charms, resting in a little bowl that Dina let her take from the kitchen.

She goes to lie back down on the bed.

She doesn't often think about the day the necklace became hers, but lying there with nothing to do except watch the rain splatter her window, she can't keep the memory away.

It was the night of her eighth birthday. Her mother had made macaroni and cheese for dinner, and then the two of them had ice-cream sandwiches and a Sara Lee cake from the Mini-Mart. Molly remembers squeezing her eyes shut, blowing out the pink stripy candles, and wishing hard for a bicycle (pink with white and pink streamers hanging from the handlebars). Then she'd sat on the couch waiting for her dad to get home.

She remembers her mom muttering, pacing back and forth with the phone. She'd already called several times, but Molly's dad wasn't picking up his cell phone. "How could you forget your only daughter's birthday?" she hissed into the phone as if someone was actually there on the other end of the line to be yelled at.

Molly pressed herself into the couch cushions as hard as she could, wanting to disappear. Wishing it wasn't her birthday. If it wasn't her birthday, her mom wouldn't be mad and her dad wouldn't be in trouble.

The aftertaste of the sugary cake was sour in her mouth.

After a while Molly had slipped from the couch, put on her pajamas, and crawled into bed.

An hour or so later she was woken by a shake on her shoulder. Her father was sitting in the chair beside her bed, holding a plastic grocery bag. "Hey, Molly Molasses," he whispered. "You awake?"

She blinked and nodded.

"Hold out your hand."

She did, and he pulled three little cards out of the bag. On each one a small charm was wired into place. "Fishy," he said, handing her the small pearly blue-and-green fish. "Raven." The pewter bird. "Bear." A tiny brown teddy bear. "It's supposed to be a Maine black bear, but this is all they had," he said apologetically. "I was trying to figure out what I could get you for your birthday. And I was thinking. You and me are Indian. Your mom's not, but we are. So let's see if I remember this right." He moved over to sit on the bed and plucked the bird charm out of her hands. "Okay, this guy is magic. He'll protect you from bad spells and stuff." Then he picked up the teddy bear. "This fierce guy is a protector."

She laughed, relaxing. Her dad was home. Now her mom wouldn't be mad anymore. Everything was all right, and it was okay that she'd had a birthday after all.

"No, really. He may not look like much, but he's fearless. And he'll make you brave, too. All right. Now the fish. This one might be the best of all. He'll give you the power to resist other people's magic. How cool is that?"

She smiled sleepily. "But magic's not real. Just in stories."

Her father's face grew serious.

"No, there's a real kind of magic, Molly Molasses. You're old enough to know about it now." She felt a thrill that climbed up from her stomach, hearing her father say that. "It's not like bad spells. It might be stuff that looks real good and sounds real nice. It might be— oh, I don't know. Like maybe somebody telling you it's okay to steal a candy bar from the Mini-Mart. You know it's wrong to steal a candy bar, right? But maybe this person has a lot of magic and he's saying, 'Oh, come on, Moll, you won't get caught. Don't you love candy, come on, just one time?'" He wiggled the fish in his fingers and pretended that it was talking. "'No, thank you! I know what you're up to. You are not putting your magic on me, no sir, I will swim right away from you, y'hear?'"

Molly smiled. Her dad smiled back.

"But now you're protected from that sort of magic. Nobody can make you do stuff you don't want to do. Nobody can tell you who you are, nobody but you."

Two weeks later, coming home late one night, he'd died in a car crash. Her mom became too depressed to take care of her. Within six months, Molly was living with her first foster family.

There were three more families after that, including, now, Ralph and Dina.

Molly lies on her bed, thinking about her life. Thinking about bad spells and bravery and magic.

Then she goes to the garage to see if Ralph can give her a ride into town.

DOROTHY
HEMINGFORD COUNTY, MINNESOTA, 1930

When she was finally better, Dorothy rode to school with Miss Larsen. Back at Mrs. Murphy's house, she set the table for breakfast, cleared the plates, swept the hall, and helped to wash the dishes after dinner. No one asked her to do any of these things, but she was determined to show Mrs. Murphy how useful she could be.

She told herself not to hope, but a week at the boardinghouse turned into two, then three. Maybe, Dorothy thought, Mrs. Murphy would simply forget that she didn't belong there.

But of course she didn't forget.

One afternoon, when Dorothy returned in the car with Miss Larsen from school, Mr. Sorenson was standing in the front hall with Mrs. Murphy, holding his black felt hat in front of him like a steering wheel. Dorothy's throat closed up so sharply that it hurt.

"Ah, here she is!" Mrs. Murphy exclaimed. "Come, Niamh, into the parlor. Join, us, please, Miss Larsen. Tea, Mr. Sorenson?"

Mrs. Murphy gestured toward the rose-velvet sofa, and he sat down heavily. Miss Larsen and Dorothy settled in the chairs across from it.

"Niamh again, are you?" Mr. Sorenson asked.

"I don't know." The girl glanced out of the window at the trees with their tender green leaves as Mrs. Murphy bustled back in with the rose-painted teapot on a tray.

"Let's go back to Dorothy, shall we?" he said. "Easier."

Miss Larsen looked at Dorothy, and the girl nodded. She knew there was no use pretending she had a choice.

Mr. Sorenson cleared his throat. "Why don't we get to it?" He pulled a paper out of his pocket. "There are several ways to proceed," he said. "First, we can send you back to New York. Or we can attempt to find another home." He sighed heavily. "Which, to be frank, might prove difficult. We've had two failed attempts at placing you already. Trouble with the woman of the house in both places."

Dorothy felt herself shrinking in her chair. But Miss

Larsen sat up stiffly. "Surely, Mr. Sorenson, you are not blaming Dorothy?"

Mr. Sorenson sighed. "Miss Larsen, I am merely being honest. Twice Dorothy has been . . . asked to leave a home. Regardless of who was truly to blame, this complicates a third placement."

Dorothy knew this was true. It didn't matter if the Byrnes went bankrupt or if Mrs. Grote never wanted her at all. All a new family would see is a girl who was told to leave. Twice.

"Mr. Sorenson, surely there's a family—" Miss Larsen began.

He held up a hand. "Miss Larsen, please. Let me finish. Mrs. Murphy has brought something to my attention. A couple named the Nielsens, friends of hers, own the general store on Center Street. Five years ago they lost their only child."

"Diphtheria, I believe it was, poor thing," said Mrs. Murphy.

"Yes, yes, tragedy," said Mr. Sorenson. "Well, apparently they've been looking for help with the shop."

Mrs. Murphy poured more tea into Mr. Sorenson's cup. "I told Mrs. Nielsen about you, Niamh. I said that you are a sober-minded girl, ten years old, and mature for your age. I have no doubt you can be of use to her. And so they have agreed to meet with you."

Dorothy knew she was expected to say something. She raised the corners of her mouth into a smile.

"How kind of Mrs. Murphy!" Miss Larsen exclaimed. "That's wonderful news, isn't it, Dorothy?"

"Yes. Thank you, Mrs. Murphy," Dorothy said, choking out the words.

Chapter Eighteen

MOLLY
SPRUCE HARBOR, MAINE, PRESENT DAY

With cold rain pelting the hood of her jacket, Molly stands on the sidewalk in front of the Spruce Harbor Library. Behind her, Ralph pulls away from the curb. He said he'd be back to pick her up in an hour and a half.

Maybe this isn't such a good idea. Molly is tempted to go get a soda at the Rite-Aid and just wait for Ralph to come back. She checks her pockets. Darn. Only a quarter and a nickel.

The rain is the kind of persistent downpour that finds every weak point in your jacket, drips down your neck, soaks your jeans from the hems up. Molly's shoes are already wet.

She's getting soaked. She needs shelter. And anyway, she's sick of feeling like a coward.

She heads toward the library doors and shoves them open.

Maybe, she thinks, *Mrs. LeBlanc isn't working today.* Then Molly can just sit down at one of the computers and get to work. But of course she doesn't have that kind of luck. The first person she sees when she walks into the library is Mrs. LeBlanc behind the checkout desk.

Mrs. LeBlanc sees Molly too. She narrows her eyes.

There are two computer terminals on a table to the right of the checkout desk. Both are occupied. A boy, probably high school age, is playing a game. An older woman with stiff permed hair is energetically typing.

Molly spots a piece of paper taped to the wall above the monitors. It says "Computer sign-up sheet at the front desk. Two hours maximum. No exceptions!"

Great. Now she'll have to go right up to the desk. If Mrs. LeBlanc hadn't already spotted her, Molly would be tempted to turn around and leave, no matter how wet she'd get. But that would make her look like a total idiot.

Her stomach flopping inside her like a fish on a line, Molly walks up to the desk.

"Um," she said. Her voice comes out as a squeak. She clears her throat. "Can I sign up for a computer?"

Mrs. LeBlanc has smooth black hair, cut just a little longer than Molly's, with a few strands of silvery white. She's wearing heavy silver earrings and a blue blouse the color of the sea. She nods at the sheet on a clipboard by her elbow.

Molly picks up a ballpoint pen and writes her name. Is she imagining it, or is Mrs. LeBlanc eyeing her backpack? She's tempted to slink over to the computers and wait her turn. But then she thinks of the charms from her father. *Bad spells. Bravery. Magic.*

"I'm sorry," she blurts. She meets Mrs. LeBlanc's eyes and notices that they are a clear green behind her glasses. "About the book. I really am. I won't . . . I mean, you don't have to worry about that. Anymore."

Mrs. LeBlanc gives her a measured smile. "Well, Molly, I appreciate your apology," she says. "It's not easy to do that." A tiny hint of respect seems to have crept into her voice.

Molly smiles back. "Thank you."

"You have a community service assignment, I hear. How's that going?"

"I'm almost done with the twenty hours."

"Then we can consider the matter closed, I think." Molly's stomach settles down. "Are you here for schoolwork? Or for yourself?"

"Something for school," Molly says. "A history report."

"Well, a computer's free now." Mrs. LeBlanc points

at the teenage boy walking away. "Can I help you find anything?"

Molly tugs a notebook out of her backpack. "There's this ship . . . it came here from Ireland. I was hoping to find a picture of it."

"What year?"

Molly flips the notebook open to check the date. "Nineteen twenty-nine."

"Well, then." Mrs. LeBlanc stands up and steps out from behind the desk. "Let's get started."

Molly sits down at the computer, and Mrs. LeBlanc pulls up a chair beside her. "This ship . . . did it dock at Ellis Island?"

"I think so."

"All right. Let's begin with the website for the Ellis Island Museum."

Mrs. LeBlanc helps Molly find a section called the Passenger Search. "You'll be fine from here, I think," she says. "Come back to the desk if you need more help."

After she leaves, Molly finds a *Ship Search* button. She clicks it, checks her notebook, and types "Agnes Pauline."

The screen opens to a long list of passengers. Molly scrolls down, reading the names. And then she nearly jumps in her seat: there they are, Vivian's parents. *Patrick and Mary Power from County Galway.* It's as if characters in a book suddenly walked off the page, as if Mary or Dickon greeted her by name, as if Anne waved to her on the street or Mrs. Lynde leaned over from the next computer to peer at her screen.

She tries something else—"Patrick and Mary Power Fire Elizabeth Street 1929."

On a site about tenement life in New York City, there's a picture of an old newspaper with an article about a fire. Patrick and Mary Power and their twin sons, Dominick and James, perished.

There's no mention of Maisie.

That's odd. Maisie died in the fire too. Why wouldn't the newspaper article say anything about her? Molly clicks back to the Ellis Island site and looks up the passenger records again to make sure she's spelling the names right. Patrick and Mary Power and their four children—Niamh, Dominick, James, and Margaret.

Margaret. Maisie's real name was Margaret. Molly types some more, but she can't find any additional information about Margaret Power who died in a fire in 1929.

She thinks back to other names from Vivian's stories. Maybe she can find out what happened to Miss Larsen? It wouldn't be just for her project, either. Vivian would like to know. It would be like a present Molly could bring her.

But Molly doesn't know the teacher's first name. She'll have to ask Vivian.

Molly flips through the pages in her notebook, searching for other names. What about those neighbors, the ones on Elizabeth Street, the ones who took Niamh in after the fire? The Schatzmans? Maybe the tenement site will have something.

She types in "Schatzman Elizabeth Street New York 1929."

A new page pops up. Someone named Liza Schatzman organized a family reunion in upstate New York a few years ago and created a page of family photographs. One is a brownish-colored print of a stern-looking man and a smiling woman with a little girl on her lap.

The caption below says "Agneta and Bernard Schatzman and their daughter, Margaret. Photo taken at their home, 29 Elizabeth Street, New York. Margaret's original family died in a tragic fire when she was very young, and she was not expected to survive. But those of us who know Margaret won't be surprised to hear that she didn't give up easily. When she came home from the hospital, very much alive against all odds, Agneta and Bernard adopted her as their own in 1930."

Molly sits back in her chair. Maisie!

Maisie didn't die in the hospital. Maisie survived the fire. And when she came home, the Schatzmans took her in.

Molly types frantically. Margaret Schatzman. Maisie Schatzman. The same family reunion page gives her what she's looking for—a photograph of a white-haired woman, eighty-two years old. Margaret Reynolds. Maiden name Schatzman. She's surrounded by children, grandchildren, great-grandchildren, at her home in Rhinebeck, New York.

Maisie lived her whole life not eight hours away from Spruce Harbor.

What else can Molly find out? She types eagerly. "Margaret Reynolds, Rhinebeck NY."

A newspaper article pops up. Molly's heart, beating fast, suddenly plummets right down to her toes.

Mrs. Margaret Reynolds, age 83, died peacefully in her sleep on Saturday after a short illness. She was surrounded by her loving family. . . .

The article goes on, but Molly doesn't want to read it. Maisie survived the fire, but she didn't survive her eighth decade. She's dead for real this time.

Molly is surprised at how terribly sad she feels.

She leaves her computer and dashes over to the desk to find Mrs. LeBlanc again. "Can I print something?" she asks breathlessly.

Mrs. LeBlanc nods. "A dime a page."

Molly digs in the pockets of her jeans, pulls out the quarter and nickel, plops them on the counter, and hurries back to her computer. She prints three pages from the site that show the pictures of Maisie and her family.

But she isn't sure what to do with them.

She doesn't want to upset Vivian. Should she show her the pictures? For that matter, should she tell Vivian about Maisie at all?

Chapter Nineteen

MOLLY
SPRUCE HARBOR, MAINE, PRESENT DAY

It's Monday night, and Molly is doing a sheet of math problems at the kitchen table. Actually, what she's doing is staring at her paper and thinking about Margaret Reynolds. Maisie Power. Her discovery at the library the day before sits in her stomach like a stone.

She wishes she could ask somebody for advice. But who? Ralph? Lori? It doesn't seem right to tell anyone else before she tells Vivian. *If* she tells Vivian.

If only she could call Jack, but Jack's still mad at her. That afternoon, he walked past her lunch table again without a word. She pokes her pencil at the paper and snaps the point right off.

Ralph comes into the kitchen, headed for the refrigerator. "Math?" he asks, looking over Molly's shoulder. "I hated that."

"That's why I do the budget," Dina says from the sink, where she's running water over the dinner dishes.

"So how's it going? Moll? Earth to Molly?" Ralph asks.

She looks up. "Okay." She pulls her backpack out from under the table and digs through it, taking out books and folders and stacking them on the table.

"What's that?" Dina says sharply. She has turned around and is wiping her hands on a dish towel.

"What?"

Dina takes two steps over to the table to snatch a book from the pile. "Where'd you get this?" she demands, waving *Anne of Green Gables* in Molly's face.

Molly's stomach sinks. She'd forgotten the book was in there.

"Molly?" Ralph is looking worried.

She sits up straight. "Vivian gave it to me."

Dina flips through the book. "Says right here it belongs to Dorothy Power. Who's that?"

Molly opens her mouth and shuts it again, dumb-struck by how complicated it's going to be to explain who Dorothy is.

Dina turns to Ralph. "She stole from the library, and now she's stealing from that old lady—or from some-body else, maybe. Some kid at school."

Molly looks at Ralph. "I did not steal that book."

He runs a hand through his hair. "It does look kind of bad, Molly."

"Kind of bad?" Dina snorts.

"You can call Vivian!" Molly insists. "Ask her. She'll tell you."

"Ralph, I can't put up with this." Dina raises her voice. "I told you one more problem and she's—"

"Dina, calm down." Ralph interrupts, his tone so firm that both Molly and Dina are startled. Dina closes her mouth so abruptly that Molly can actually hear the click of her teeth.

But Molly can finish Dina's sentence for herself.

She's out.

Molly gets up and heads for her room, leaving the book on the table and Dina and Ralph glaring at each other.

In her bedroom, Molly hauls her L.L.Bean duffel bags out from under the bed. She opens dresser drawers and scoops up socks and underwear, dumping them on the floor by the bags. T-shirts next. Jeans. She can hear voices from the kitchen, but she's not listening to the words.

She knows what they're saying already. Dina insisting that Molly has to go. Ralph giving in. There will be phone calls, discussions, arrangements. She's heard it all before.

Molly grabs shoes from under the bed—purple flip-flops, a pair of black sneakers from Walmart—and sets them in the bottom of the red duffel bag. She's learned to put heavy stuff on the bottom. It will keep her things neat and in order. Everything where it should be.

She rolls her black jeans and black T-shirts and puts them carefully in place. Whatever happens, she'll be packed and ready.

But she'll never get done with her portaging project, never finish her hours in Vivian's attic. Will she get to say good-bye to her? And what about Jack? Is she going to leave town with her one friend still mad at her?

Sitting on the floor by her duffel, Molly tugs her phone out of her pocket. She wants to call Jack . . . but what would she say? Apologize? Ask for help? Explain that she's about to get kicked out and only called to say good-bye?

She can't do it.

Suddenly she remembers the necklace. She drops the phone in the duffel and darts across the room. Maybe she's going to leave her friend behind, but the charms have to come with her. She picks the necklace up from its little dish and clasps it carefully around her neck. Her throat aches fiercely. But she's not going to cry. She never cries.

"She didn't steal it, Dina."

Ralph's voice comes through Molly's door so loudly and clearly that she sits on her bed in surprise.

"Mrs. Daly says she gave the book to Molly. Molly didn't steal anything."

"Well . . ." Molly hears Dina sputter. "She stole that other book!"

"She made a mistake, and she's paying for it. People deserve second chances. We took her in, Deen. We made a commitment to her. I want her to know she has a home she can count on."

There's a knock on Molly's door. "Come in," she says.

Ralph stands in the doorway, looking in at the packed duffel bag on the floor, at Molly sitting rigidly on the bed.

"Hey," he says gently. "What are you doing?"

The ache in her throat is so sharp she can't speak.

Ralph comes over to sit beside her. "You don't have to pack up," he says. "I called Vivian. She says she did give you that book."

"I told you," Molly whispers.

"Yeah. You did." Ralph nods. "Molly, I want you to stay here. With us. We hope you will."

"'We'?" Molly says. "Yeah, right."

Dina is in the doorway now with *Anne of Green Gables* in her hands. Her eyes are oddly bright. She blinks hard. "Here," she says, and walks over to hand Molly the book. "I'm sorry I jumped to conclusions."

She looks at the half-packed duffel. "Don't leave that stuff all over the floor," she says. "It's a mess. Put it away before you go to bed, okay?"

Ralph smiles at Molly and gives her a little wink. She smiles back. "Okay," she says.

Chapter Twenty

MOLLY
SPRUCE HARBOR, MAINE, PRESENT DAY

That's it, Molly thinks. *Done.*

Standing quietly with Vivian, she looks around at the attic.

Every single item in every single box has been taken out, dusted off, and discussed. A few things were thrown out, a few more brought downstairs to be used. But most of the stuff stayed right where it was.

The attic is clean. Just not cleaned out.

Molly recycled some of the boxes that were old and crumpled or torn. Terry got her new, sturdy ones, and then Molly rewrapped and refolded and repacked everything Vivian wanted to keep. She labeled it all by place and date with a new black Sharpie and taped a list from her notebook on each box to show what was inside.

If Vivian ever needs to find anything now, she'll know right where to look.

"Mission accomplished," Vivian says, nodding.

It seems to Molly that something more should be said. It wasn't just Vivian's attic they went through. It was her whole life.

"How about a cup of tea?" Vivian turns and makes her way down the staircase. Molly follows.

When Terry brings a tray into the living room, Molly is happy to see, instead of the usual thick white mugs, the fragile flowered teacups and teapot she and Vivian found in the attic. Vivian fills a cup with amber tea for herself and another for Molly.

"So you're done up there?" Terry asks.

Molly nods, a little nervous. But Vivian gives Terry a big smile. "It's just as I want it to be," she says firmly.

Terry shakes her head a little. "You're the boss, Vivi," she says, and goes back to the kitchen.

Vivian turns her eyes on Molly. "I'll sign those papers for you," she says. "You put in more than twenty hours. And do you have any more questions for me?"

Molly thinks about Maisie. She still doesn't know whether it would do more harm than good to tell Vivian the news. For now, at least, she decides to keep quiet. Besides, there is something she wants to know. She sets her cup in its saucer, careful to do it gently so the tea won't slosh or the porcelain won't crack, and digs her recorder out of her backpack. "What about the

Nielsens? What happened with them? You have to finish the story!"

Vivian smiles and leans back in her chair, her own teacup still in her hand. "I'm glad you want to know."

"Did you meet them? What were they like?"

"Yes, I met them. Mr. Sorenson came back, and Mr. and Mrs. Nielsen came with him."

DOROTHY
HEMINGFORD COUNTY, MINNESOTA, 1930

Dorothy greeted Mr. and Mrs. Nielsen in Mrs. Murphy's parlor while Mr. Sorenson and Miss Larsen stood quietly behind them.

Mr. Nielsen, Dorothy thought, looked like a large gray mouse. He even had the twitching whiskers. Mrs. Nielsen was frail. Her dark hair was pulled back in a bun and her lips were painted with dark red lipstick.

Mrs. Murphy poured tea and handed them a plate full of biscuits. First they chatted about what kind of winter it had been and how lovely it was to feel the warmth of spring. Then they started asking questions. "What are your special skills, Dorothy?"

"I can sew, and I'm quite neat. I'm good with

numbers," she told them.

Mr. Nielsen, turning to Mrs. Murphy, asked, "And can the young lady cook and clean?"

"Of course. She is a hardworking girl, I can tell you that," Mrs. Murphy said.

"Does she go to church?" Mrs. Nielsen asked.

Dorothy remembered clasping her gran's hand as they walked to St. Joseph's, right in the center of Kinvara. The smell of incense and lilies. But Da didn't hold with religion, and when they moved to New York, Mam couldn't manage to pack up four children by herself on a Sunday morning. Dorothy hadn't been to church since leaving the village.

She wasn't sure how to answer Mrs. Nielsen's question.

"She's an Irish girl, Viola, so I imagine she's Catholic," Mr. Nielsen said.

Dorothy nodded.

"Well, we will expect you to go to Lutheran service with us on Sundays," Mrs. Nielsen said.

Dorothy nodded again. One hour of Protestant church on Sundays was a small price to pay, she supposed, for a safe place to stay. The Nielsens looked respectable. Perhaps there would actually be a warm bed, food to eat, clothes to wear.

Of course, Mr. and Mrs. Byrne had looked respectable too. Dorothy knew better than to put too much faith in what she saw.

"We will send you to school in town here, a short walk from our house—so you won't attend Miss Larsen's class any longer," Mrs. Nielsen said.

Miss Larsen said, "I believe Dorothy was about to outgrow the schoolhouse anyway. She's such a smart girl."

"And in the afternoons after school," Mr. Nielsen said, "you will be expected to help in the store. We'll pay you an hourly wage, of course. You know about the store, Dorothy, do you not?"

Dorothy nodded and nodded and nodded.

The next morning, Mr. Nielsen pulled up in a blue-and-white Studebaker with silver trim.

Mrs. Murphy had gone through her trunks and her attic, and now Dorothy had two suitcases full of clothes and shoes. Miss Larsen pressed a green hardcover book—*Anne of Green Gables*—into her hands. "It's my own book, not the school's, and I want you to have it," she said as she hugged Dorothy good-bye.

And so, for the fourth time since she set foot in Minnesota, everything Dorothy owned was loaded into a vehicle and she was on her way to somewhere new.

"And that's all?" asks Molly.

"All?" Vivian sets her teacup down. "Well, no, not quite. I was only ten years old, you know. I've lived more than eighty years since then. But in some ways, I suppose it is the end of the story. That story, anyway."

"Were they nice, the Nielsens? Did you end up with them for good? They didn't sound all that nice," Molly says.

"They didn't? Well, actually they were. Quiet people, yes. Never very . . . demonstrative, do you know what that means? They didn't show much of what they felt. But they were decent and kind, in their own way. We got used to each other slowly, and eventually I believe we even came to love each other. After all I'd been through, it was enough."

Molly can understand that. Sometimes you don't look for perfect. Sometimes *enough* is the most you can hope for.

Maybe that's what she'll get at Ralph and Dina's. She's not sure. A week has passed since the big argument over the book and Dina's apology. Things are better between them, for sure. Dina has been friendlier, and Ralph seems relieved. A few days ago, they came to Molly together to tell her she was welcome to stay.

The question is, does she want to?

Maybe Dina will never be Molly's favorite person. Maybe Molly will never be Dina's, either. But if she stays at their house, she'll still be in Spruce Harbor. Where she might be able to make a new friend or two—like Megan. Where she can patch things up with Jack, the friend she already has. And where she can still come and see Vivian.

After all Molly's been through, maybe it's enough.

"Several years after the Nielsens took me in, they adopted me," Vivian goes on. "They had already asked if I'd change my name to the name of their daughter who'd died."

"Vivian," Molly says.

"That's right. Vivian."

"And didn't you mind?" Molly can't imagine Ralph or Dina asking if she'd change the name she's had all her life, the name her father gave her. No more Molly Molasses?

"Well, I didn't have much reason to be attached to the name Dorothy," Vivian says. "And I knew they wouldn't go for Niamh. I think it gave Mrs. Nielsen some comfort to give me that name."

"And you worked in the store for them?" Molly asks.

Vivian nods. "I was quite good at it, as a matter of

fact. Doing the accounts, the ordering. I became an expert at watching people, at guessing what they might want. Mr. Nielsen came to rely on me very much. Once I graduated from high school, I managed the store. And when they died, they left everything to me. My husband and I ran it together until we decided to retire."

Molly's head is spinning a little. She's been so deep into Vivian's story, imagining the life of that girl traveling on a train, going from one family to the next, carrying her few possessions with her like a Wabanaki used to, that she'd almost forgotten that a lot has happened to Vivian since then.

"Did you ever hear anything about any of the other children on the train?" she asks. "Like Carmine? Or Dutchy?"

"Carmine . . . no, I never heard anything about him. But Dutchy?" She lets out a big sigh.

"What?"

"Goodness, yes, child, I thought I told you."

Molly shakes her head.

"Well, it will be one last thing to add to your report. When I was nineteen, I went into Minneapolis with two of my friends to see *The Wizard of Oz*. I'd never seen a motion picture in color before."

"Never?" Molly asks.

"Don't look so surprised. Color movies were very

rare back then." Vivian looks away, into the distance, at something Molly can't see. "You've seen movies in color since before you could talk. But it was magical to me."

It doesn't seem foolish to Molly at all. She can imagine how it must've felt, walking out of that theater—as if Oz could be right around the corner. As if the gray, ordinary world might vanish any second, and a world of color open up.

"After the movie I was sitting in the lobby of a hotel, waiting for my friends," Vivian goes on. "And a man walked by. He stopped and looked at me. I noticed his eyes. They were very blue. Startling. He asked if he knew me from somewhere."

"So did you know him?" Molly asks.

"I didn't think so, not at first. It wasn't normal, you know, for a man to just stop and talk to a woman like that. I was annoyed. I thought he was going to be a bother, and that I'd have to go to the hotel desk and ask someone to escort him out. But then he asked if I had traveled from New York to Minnesota on a train when I was young. And he called me Niamh. It had been so long since anyone used that name, I almost couldn't answer."

Molly sits up straight. "Was it—Vivian, was it Dutchy?"

She gives Molly a broad smile. "Yes. It was Dutchy."

"What had happened to him?" Molly asks. "Did he get adopted? Were those people who took him off the train as awful as they seemed?"

"Quite as awful, I'm sorry to say," Vivian answers. "He ran away. He was taken in by another farmer, a much kinder man. By the time I met Dutchy in the hotel lobby that night, he'd become a musician. He played the piano, in bars or nightclubs, mostly."

"And you got to be friends with him?" Molly asks. "You stayed in touch and everything?"

"A little more than that," Vivian answers. "We were married ten months later. Mrs. Murphy gave me a tea set just like hers for a wedding present."

Molly stares in astonishment. "You married him!"

"I married him. He was the only one who understood, you see, just what my life had been like. That is, until you came to clean out my attic."

Vivian smiles, running a finger around the rim of her teacup with its blooming red roses.

Molly smiles back.

"I've never told anyone else about my early life," Vivian continues. "I didn't even tell the Nielsens. We didn't discuss things much in those days. Nowadays people talk about everything. There are therapists and counselors and all that." Vivian shakes her head as if it's too much to understand. "But when I was young, we just got on with things. The Nielsens didn't ask me much, and I didn't tell them. And then, eight decades later, you come along, with your blue hair and your black fingernails and that little recorder of yours. I never could have imagined that you'd be the one I'd tell."

Molly feels a glow of happiness, but it quickly fades. Something feels wrong, and after a moment, she realizes what it is.

Vivian's story will never be complete until she knows about Maisie. Molly is going to have to figure out a way to tell her. But before that, there's something else she needs to get off her chest.

Chapter Twenty-One

MOLLY
SPRUCE HARBOR, MAINE, PRESENT DAY

Molly hopes the bear charm on her necklace will give her courage. She needs it now, even more than she needed it when she walked into the library and saw Mrs. LeBlanc at the desk.

"There's something I should have told you when I met you," she says to Vivian. "The community service thing wasn't for school, not really."

"Oh?" Vivian lifts her eyebrows.

"I stole something." The words are stiff and heavy as Molly forces them out of her mouth. "A book. From the library."

"I see."

"It was a stupid thing to do," Molly admits.

"What book was it?"

She looks at Vivian in surprise. This is not what she expected her to ask. "Um. *The Secret Garden*."

"Did Terry know?"

Molly hesitates. She doesn't want to get Terry into trouble. If she does, there's no way Jack will ever forgive her. "I think—Terry asked you—because Jack asked her," she says slowly, feeling her way. "To help me out. You know how she feels about Jack."

"That I do."

"I'm not a thief," Molly says suddenly, urgently. She can't read the expression on Vivian's face. Is she angry? Disgusted? Does she think Molly is a terrible person? "I mean, I guess I am, but I gave the book back." No, she needs to be absolutely truthful here. "They took it back, really. But I've never stolen anything else, not even a bar of candy." Maybe her dad's charms saved her from that sort of thing. "But I'm sorry I didn't tell you before."

"Hmm. Well. Perhaps it was for the best," Vivian says thoughtfully. "I probably wouldn't have agreed to let you help me, had I known, and then look at all I would have missed." She studies Molly, the old sharp interest back in her eyes. "*The Secret Garden*? I know that book. Yes. A girl and a boy. Dreadful little children. Both practically orphans, like you and me."

"Don't you . . . mind?" Molly asks nervously.

Vivian lifts her shoulders. "You've certainly paid your dues. All those hours in the attic. And . . . before you even got here, I expect." She smiles. "I think we should forget all about it."

Molly smiles back, feeling a wave of relief wash over her. But she knows the time has come to tell Vivian the rest of the story.

She takes a deep breath. "There's something else I need to say."

"Oh, Lord." Vivian takes a sip of cold tea and sets her cup down. "What have you done now?"

"It's not about me," Molly says. "It's about Maisie."

Vivian's hand freezes on her flowery teacup. "Maisie?"

Molly's heart is beating quickly and shallowly, like a rabbit's. Will this news upset Vivian? Make her angry? Will she think Molly was poking her nose into something that was none of her business? Well, it's too late to stop now. "I went online," Molly says, the words coming out in a rush. "I just wanted to see if I could find something, pictures really, for my project. I found stuff from Ellis Island, the ship you were on from Ireland—"

"The *Agnes Pauline.*"

"Uh-huh." Molly looks at her own fingers on the arm of her chair, keeping her eyes away from Vivian. "And I saw a newspaper article about the fire. About your mom and dad and brothers dying. But it didn't say anything about Maisie. So I kept looking, and then . . . then I . . ."

"What, child? For goodness' sake. Just tell me."

"The Schatzmans," Molly says. "There was a family reunion site, and a picture. The Schatzmans adopted a baby. In 1930. Her name was Margaret."

"Margaret."

Molly nods.

"Maisie," Vivian breathes. "She didn't die in the fire?"

Molly nods again. Now that she's started, she has to tell the rest of it quickly. She can't let Vivian begin to hope. "But she—I'm really sorry, Vivian. She died six months ago. She was eighty-three."

Vivian is very still.

"It said—that family reunion website said—that everybody was surprised she lived after the fire. When she was a baby. The doctors and all. But she got better, and then there was no one, I guess, no family, and . . ."

"And they adopted her. The Schatzmans."

Molly nods. "Yes. I'm sorry. But she lived a long time. She had children and grandchildren and all that."

"All these years," Vivian says, very softly. "All these years she was alive, and I didn't know it."

"She looked happy," Molly says, tentatively. She reaches down into her backpack, lying at her feet, and pulls out the pages she printed at the library. She unfolds them gently and holds them out to Vivian. "See? She really does. I think she had a happy life."

Vivian drops her eyes to the pages. She's silent for a moment, then she murmurs, "Yes. I see. Yes, you're right. She does look happy."

Slowly, she puts out a finger to touch the face of her sister, lost—and found—and lost again.

Molly stacks the pages of her report in the middle of her desk, making sure all the edges are perfectly aligned. She puts a staple neatly through the upper left-hand corner.

Her portaging project is finished.

She typed up all of Vivian's memories, the ones on the recorder, the ones she wrote down in her notebook. Elizabeth Street. The fire. The train. The Byrnes and the Grotes, Miss Larsen and Mrs. Murphy. The Nielsens. Dutchy. She went back to the library once more, and Mrs. LeBlanc helped her find pictures to add: the *Agnes Pauline*, Elizabeth Street, a train full of orphans just like Vivian and Dutchy, heading out of New York City to the Midwest.

But Molly didn't put anything in her report about how Maisie survived the fire. That part is just for Vivian.

And now she's finished and will turn it in tomorrow. Molly pats the papers gently. It's Sunday morning, and she's got the rest of the weekend to herself.

That's the problem, though. She doesn't really want to spend the whole day by herself.

Before she can decide what to do, there's a knock on her door. Molly doesn't bother to say "Come in." Dina always opens the door right after she knocks.

She does it this time. Standing in the doorway, she tosses something soft in Molly's direction.

Molly grabs it out of the air.

"Saw it in the thrift shop," Dina says as Molly stares at the thing in her hands. "I thought of you."

It's the tie-dyed T-shirt with turtles swimming across the front. Blue and green, like tiny planets.

"I like turtles," Molly says in astonishment.

"I know that. Why do you think I got it?"

"I—uh." Molly can't think of anything to say. "Thanks?"

"You'll look like a hippie," Dina says with a grin, turning to leave. "But I guess that's better than looking like a vampire."

"Is it?"

"Marginally. Why don't you put it on and see if it fits?" She turns and heads for the kitchen, shutting the door behind her.

Laughing to herself, Molly gets up and tries the T-shirt on. She studies herself in the mirror. It fits perfectly.

Dina. Who would have thought? People can surprise you.

Maybe it's time Molly tries surprising somebody. After all, she had the guts to go back to the library. And to tell Vivian the truth about the book, and about Maisie.

Maybe she has the guts for this too.

She picks up her phone and dial's Jack's number. "Hey," she says when he picks up. "It's me. Molly."

"Yeah, I know." Jack sounds surprised. "It's not like I deleted your number from my phone, Moll. Just because we had a fight."

Molly isn't quite sure what to say, but she's the one who made the phone call, so she guesses it's on her. "It's a nice day out there, right?"

"You called me to talk about the weather?"

"No, I called you to ask if you want to take a hike with me," Molly says. "How about Flying Mountain?"

Chapter Twenty-Two

MOLLY
SPRUCE HARBOR, MAINE, PRESENT DAY

It's what Jack always calls a Maine postcard day: white fluffy clouds in a clear blue sky, the sea glinting in the sun, pine trees glowing a deep green, little trout lilies blooming in the shady woods. Wearing her new T-shirt, Molly sits next to Jack on a shelf of granite at the very top of the mountain, looking out to sea. "So you finished the attic?" he asks, tossing a pebble over the edge. Not looking at Molly.

"Uh-huh." Molly nods. "Vivian didn't want to get rid of much, in the end. Most of it's still up there. Just a lot neater."

Jack throws another rock.

"Listen," Molly says. "I know Terry wanted me to clean out the attic. But I think what Vivian really wanted was to see what was inside those boxes one more time. So we did that. And I'm glad. And by the way, I told her the truth."

Jack looks alarmed. "Told her what truth?"

"That I stole the book. That I wasn't just doing community service for a school project."

"Molly!" Jack groans. "What about my mom? She needs that job."

"I didn't say anything about your mom," Molly went on. "Look, Jack. Vivian is not upset about any of it. She totally understood. And the attic's finished. So . . ."

Can you stop being mad at me now? is what she really wants to ask. *Can your mom stop thinking I'm some kind of juvenile delinquent?*

To her surprise, Jack seems to be reading her mind. "Okay. I get it."

"You do?"

"Yeah. I actually think it's cool that you fessed up. I was just worried you'd get my mom in trouble."

Molly nods. "She took a risk, recommending me to Vivian."

"I should've known you'd handle it," Jack says. "You've got guts, Moll."

She smiles at him. "I'm going back over there in a few days," she says. "You can tell your mom, if you want. So she's not surprised."

"Just to hang out with Vivian?"

"She decided to get a laptop," Molly says. "She needs someone to help her set it up and teach her how to use

Google. So that's what I'm going to do."

"I'd like to see *that*," Jack says, smiling back.

Lori holds out her hand. "Let's take a look at those papers."

Molly gives her the community service forms. All her hours are dutifully filled out and dated. Vivian has signed the forms. So has Ralph.

"Impressive." Lori opens up her folder to put the community service forms away. "So look at this—a teacher put a note in here."

Molly tenses.

"Mr. Reed," Lori says. "Says you did an assignment for his class—a 'portaging project.' What's that?"

"Just a history report," Molly mumbles. "Why?" She feels a flutter of nervousness. Mr. Reed hasn't handed back their papers yet. She'd been so proud of that report—but maybe he didn't like it.

"Well, Mr. Reed says you went 'above and beyond.' He wrote that right here. Says he submitted your paper and a few other exceptional ones to the public library. That's his word, 'exceptional.' You didn't know?"

Molly sits upright, blinking. She shakes her head.

"I guess every year Mr. Reed sends a few of the best papers to Mrs. LeBlanc at the library," Lori goes on. "And they keep them in the local history section for people to read if they want to know more about Spruce Harbor. Pretty exciting, huh?" Lori smiles.

Molly feels like she's glowing.

"I'm proud of you, Molly." Lori closes her folder. "You're doing well. So stay out of trouble, okay?"

"I'll try," Molly says, grinning. "No promises. You don't want your job to get too boring, do you?"

"No chance of that," Lori says.

Vivian's new laptop has arrived. Molly shows her how to turn it on and open the web browser. She bookmarks the *New York Times* and sets up an e-mail account. "You can send me an email when you want me to come over," she tells Vivian.

"Old school," says Jack, looking over their shoulders. "You should just message each other."

"Let's not get ahead of ourselves," Vivian says. "Touchpad . . . what's the touchpad again? Oh, I see."

Molly explains how to use the search engine, and before she knows it, they're pulling up one site after another about the orphan train riders.

Some of the two hundred and fifty thousand children who rode the train are still alive. There are books and newspaper articles, plays and events. There's a website where riders can tell their stories and post photographs, as well as links to historical records and archives.

Vivian gasps.

"What is it?" asks Molly.

"I think," Vivian murmurs, leaning close to the screen. "I think I may have just found Carmine."

"Who's Carmine?" Jack asks.

"A boy Vivian knew growing up," Molly tells him. "Where, Vivian?" Vivian is looking at a black-and-white photograph of a dark-haired toddler, his arms thrown wide, a beaming smile on his face. The caption says *Carmine Luten—Minnesota—1929*.

"They didn't change his name?" Molly asks.

"Apparently not," Vivian says. "Look—here's the woman who took him out of my arms that day." She points to the screen at a picture of a slight, pretty woman standing next to a tall, thin man. Carmine, with his dark curly hair and crossed eyes, nestles between them. Farther down the page there's a picture of him on his wedding day, his eyes no longer crossed. He's wearing glasses and beaming beside a chestnut-haired girl as they cut a big white cake.

There's a paragraph about his life. Molly reads it eagerly. He became a salesman, like his adoptive father. He had one child, a son. He lived in Minnesota his whole life and died peacefully at the age of seventy-four.

"So Carmine was happy," Vivian says, nodding. "Good."

The page was created by Carmine's son. Molly goes to Facebook and types in his name—Carmine Luten Jr. There's only one in Minnesota. "I can set up an account for you if you want," she tells Vivian. "You could send his son a friend request or a message."

Vivian peers at the Facebook picture of the younger Carmine with his wife and grandchildren on what looks like a vacation to Disney World. "Goodness. I'm not quite ready for that. Later, maybe. If I decide to do it, would you help me?"

Molly feels a wide smile spreading across her face. "Of course I will."

"I got what you asked for at the supermarket," Dina says. "But I don't know if we can keep doing this. Buying all these fancy vegetables could eat up my salary pretty quick."

Molly is in the kitchen with Ralph and Dina, chopping mushrooms and peppers on the cutting board. There's a pile of grated cheese next to the vegetables and a stack of tortillas on the counter. She offered to cook dinner, thinking that if Dina actually tries a few meals that don't have a big hunk of meat in them, she'll see that being a vegetarian isn't so weird. So tonight it's quesadillas. Molly learned how to make them from a teenaged girl in her last foster home.

"Come on, Dina," Ralph says calmly, reaching over Molly's shoulder to take a pinch of the shredded cheese. "Meat's a lot more expensive than this stuff. And it looks pretty good to me. What do we do next, Moll?"

"You heat the butter on the griddle and then you put a tortilla on and fill it up with whatever you want," Molly tells him. "And you put another tortilla on top." She shows him with one for herself. Cheese and mushrooms.

After a few minutes Ralph lifts the quesadilla off the griddle, golden brown, with melted cheese dripping out of the sides.

Molly remembers how she used to fry eggs with her father, standing on a stool so she could see over the top of the skillet, holding a big black plastic spatula. "Not so fast, Molly Molasses," he'd say. "Easy. Otherwise the eggs'll go splat."

Molly takes a quesadilla over to the table, where Dina is sitting, and slides it onto her plate. Dina looks at it suspiciously and takes a bite.

"Cheese and tomatoes and peppers," Ralph says. "Good, huh?"

Dina chews and swallows. "It's actually not bad," she says with surprise.

"What should we make this weekend?" Ralph asks Molly. "How about pizza? As long as I get to add pepperoni to my half."

"I'm up for it," Molly says. "By the way, Megan asked me to come over to do homework at her house tomorrow."

"Okay. So why don't we do something fun tonight. How about a movie?"

"We could just watch Netflix at home, maybe," Molly suggests. And then she's surprised at herself. When did she start thinking of Ralph and Dina's place as home?

She's never even told them for sure that she wants to stay. But somehow they're all assuming it. And that's okay with her. Sure, it's not a perfect family. Dina and Ralph don't exactly feel like a mother and father. But Ralph is funny, and she and Dina are starting to get along. As Vivian would say, "It's enough."

"Netflix!" Ralph says scornfully. "Don't be so boring. We should see something on a big screen."

"Fine," Dina says. "I get to vote on the movie, though. Hey, can you make me another one of those cheese things, Moll?"

Molly looks over at Dina's plate. She's eaten her entire quesadilla. "You liked it, huh?"

"It was better than I thought. This time add some mushrooms, though."

"Sure thing."

Molly moves back to the cutting board. She and Ralph get to work. Soon the griddle is sizzling and there's another plateful of quesadillas ready for the table. The kitchen smells of melting cheese and frying onions, a rich, warm smell, and Molly's mouth is watering. She brings Dina a tortilla loaded with cheese and mushrooms and peppers and slides one onto her own plate.

Dina takes a huge bite and smiles at her.

Molly could get used to this. Yes, it's beginning to feel like home.

Orphan Train Girl Short History

Orphan Train Girl highlights a little-known but historically significant moment in our country's past. Between 1854 and 1929, so-called "orphan trains" transported more than two hundred and fifty thousand orphaned, abandoned, and homeless children—many of whom, like Vivian Daly, were first-generation Irish-Catholic immigrants—from the coastal cities of the

Photograph courtesy of the Library of Congress Prints & Photographs Online Catalog, Lewis Wickes Hines Collection of the National Child Labor Committee

Elizabeth Street in New York City, where Niamh lived, in the early twentieth century.

A bootblack like Dutchy, near City Hall Park, New York City, 1924.

A group of early-twentieth-century orphan train riders with their chaperones.

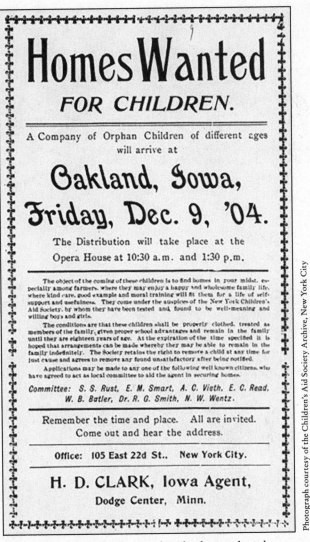

Homes Wanted

FOR CHILDREN.

A Company of Orphan Children of different ages
will arrive at

Oakland, Iowa,
Friday, Dec. 9, '04.

The Distribution will take place at the
Opera House at 10:30 a.m. and 1:30 p.m.

The object of the coming of these children is to find homes in your midst, especially among farmers, where they may enjoy a happy and wholesome family life, where kind care, good example and moral training will fit them for a life of self-support and usefulness. They come under the auspices of the *New York Children's Aid Society*, by whom they have been tested and found to be well-meaning and willing boys and girls.

The conditions are that these children shall be properly clothed, treated as members of the family, given proper school advantages and remain in the family until they are eighteen years of age. At the expiration of the time specified it is hoped that arrangements can be made whereby they may be able to remain in the family indefinitely. The Society retains the right to remove a child at any time for just cause and agrees to remove any found unsatisfactory after being notified.

Applications may be made to any one of the following well known citizens, who have agreed to act as local committee to aid the agent in securing homes.

*Committee: S. S. Rust, E. M. Smart, A. C. Vieth, E. C. Read,
W. B. Batler, Dr. R. G. Smith, N. W. Wentz.*

Remember the time and place. All are invited.
Come out and hear the address.

Office: 105 East 22d St., New York City.

H. D. CLARK, Iowa Agent,
Dodge Center, Minn.

*Notices like this one were posted in the days and weeks
before a train arrived in town.*

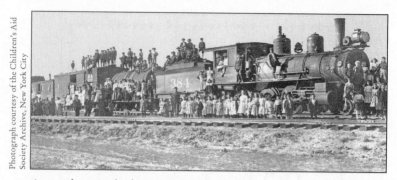

A rare photograph of an entire train of children on its way to Kansas.

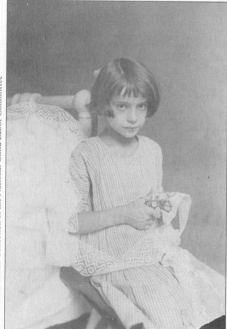

A young girl like Niamh/Dorothy, sewing to earn money.

eastern United States to the Midwest. These children were indentured or contracted, which meant that they were expected to work without pay until the age of eighteen or twenty-one. Charles Loring Brace, who founded the program, believed that hard work, education, and firm but compassionate child rearing—not to mention Midwestern Christian family values—were the only way to save these children from a life of sin and poverty. Until the late 1930s, there were no government programs like welfare and foster care; it is estimated that more than ten thousand children were living on the streets of New York City at any given time.

Many of the children had experienced great trauma in their short lives, and they had no idea where they were going. The train would pull into a station and the local townspeople would assemble to inspect them—often closely examining teeth, eyes, and limbs to determine whether a child was sturdy enough for fieldwork, or intelligent and mild-tempered enough to cook and clean. Babies and healthy older boys were typically chosen first; older girls were chosen last. After a brief trial period, the children became indentured or contracted to their host families. If a child wasn't chosen, he or she would get back on the train to try again at the next town.

Some children were warmly welcomed by new families and towns. Others were beaten, mistreated, taunted, or ignored. They lost any sense of their cultural identities and backgrounds; siblings were usually separated, and contact between them was discouraged. City children were expected to perform hard farm labor for which they were neither emotionally nor physically prepared. Many of them, first-generation immigrants from Italy, Poland, and Ireland, among other places, were teased for their strange accents; some barely spoke English. Jealousy and competition in the new families created rifts, and many children ended up feeling that they didn't belong anywhere. Some drifted from home to home to find someone who wanted them. Many ran away. The Children's Aid Society did attempt to keep track of these children, but the reality of great distances and spotty record keeping made this difficult.

Many train riders never spoke about their early lives. But as the years passed, some train riders and their descendants began to tell their stories. They demanded access to records that had been closed to them. One train rider I spoke with, ninety-four-year-old Pat Thiessen, told me that when, in her fifties, she finally got her birth certificate with her parents' names on it, she shouted with joy. "I was so happy to know about myself, just a little," she said. "It [still] feels incomplete. I keep wondering: What were my grandparents like? What did they have in my family that I could've enjoyed? Who would I be?"

Acknowledgments

More than a decade ago, my husband, our three boys, and I were visiting his mother in Fargo, North Dakota, for the holidays. Stuck inside during a three-day blizzard, my mother-in-law pulled a book off the shelf to read to her grandsons. It was filled with old newspaper articles from her hometown of Jamestown, North Dakota, one of which was titled, "They called it 'Orphan Train'—and it proved there was a home for many children on the prairie." Imagine my mother-in-law's surprise when she saw the photographs of her father, his brother, and their three sisters! None of us had heard of the orphan trains. Immediately I knew I wanted to learn more about this little-known period in American history.

I was stunned to learn that the orphan trains transported an estimated two hundred and fifty thousand children from the East Coast to the Midwest between 1854 and 1929, many of them new immigrants to this country. In the course of writing this book, I traveled to County Galway in Ireland to research my character's

Irish background. (I am part Irish myself.) When I learned that many train riders ended up in Minnesota, I attended train riders' reunions in New York and Minnesota, and interviewed train riders and their descendants.

Several of the small towns in Minnesota I name in this novel are invented, as is Spruce Harbor, Maine, the setting for the present-day story. (Spruce Harbor is also the setting for another of my novels, *The Way Life Should Be*.) Planting an imaginary town in a real landscape gives me freedom as a writer to invent as I go.

In the course of my research, I was lucky to meet Renee Wendinger, president of the Midwest Orphan Train Riders from New York organization, whose mother, Sophia Hillesheim, was a train rider. At the Orphan Train Riders of New York forty-ninth reunion in 2009 in Little Falls, Minnesota, Renee introduced me to half a dozen train riders, all in their nineties. She also introduced me by phone to Pat Thiessen, a train rider from Ireland whose experience uncannily resembled the one I had sketched for my character. Throughout the writing of this novel, Renee patiently and generously offered her wise counsel in ways large and small, from correcting egregious errors to providing historical nuance and shading. Her book, *Extra!*

Extra! The Orphan Trains and Newsboys of New York, has been an invaluable resource. The novel would not be the same without her.

Other resources I relied on during my research were the Children's Aid Society, the New York Foundling (I attended their 140th Homecoming in 2009 and met a number of train riders there), the New York Tenement Museum, the Ellis Island Immigration Museum, and the National Orphan Train Complex in Concordia, Kansas, a museum and research center with a vibrant online presence that includes many train rider stories. In the Irma and Paul Milstein Division of United States History, Local History and Genealogy at the New York Public Library, I found noncirculating lists of orphaned and indigent children from the Children's Aid Society and the New York Foundling, first-person testimonials from train riders and their families, handwritten records, notes from desperate mothers explaining why they abandoned their children, reports on Irish immigrants, and many other documents that aren't available anywhere else. Books I found particularly helpful include *Orphan Train Rider: One Boy's True Story*, by Andrea Warren; *Children of the Orphan Trains, 1854–1929*, by Holly Littlefield; and *Rachel Calof's Story: Jewish Homesteader on the*

Northern Plains, edited by J. Sanford Rikoon (which I found at Bonanzaville, a pioneer prairie village and museum complex in West Fargo).

Irish native Brian Nolan took me on an insider's tour of County Galway; his stories about his childhood housekeeper, Birdie Sheridan, provided inspiration for Vivian's grandmother's life. In the village of Kinvara, Robyn Richardson ferried me from pubs to Phantom Street and handed me an important resource, *Kinvara: A Seaport Town on Galway Bay* (written by Caoilte Breatnach and compiled by Anne Korff). Among other books, *An Irish Country Childhood*, by Marrie Walsh, helped me with period and place details.

At the same time that I was writing this book, my mother, Tina Baker—a professor at the University of Maine and a Maine state legislator—was teaching a class called "Native American Women in Literature and Myth." At the end of the course she asked students to use the Indian concept of portaging to describe "their journeys along uncharted waters and what they chose to carry forward in portages to come." The concept of portaging, I realized, was the missing strand I needed to weave my book together. Additional titles shaped my perspective: *Women of the Dawn*, by Bunny McBride, *In the Shadow of the Eagle: A Tribal Representative in*

Maine, by Donna M. Loring (a member of the Penobscot Indian Nation and a former state legislator herself), and *The Wabanakis of Maine and the Maritimes*, by the Wabanaki Program of the American Friends Service Committee. The websites of the Abbe Museum in Bar Harbor, Maine, and the Penobscot Indian Nation provided valuable material as well.

The Indian Child Welfare Act (ICWA) of 1978 was created as an effort to keep Native American children with Native American families because an alarming number of children were being taken from their homes and denied their cultural heritage. In a case like Molly's, when a Native American family is not available to foster a child, the Tribal Court will allow her to be fostered to a non-Indian family. I am greatly indebted to Donna Loring for reading the manuscript carefully, advising me on issues related to the ICWA, and adding shading and nuance to some complicated questions about Native American symbols and laws. Julia Gray at the Abbe Museum in Bar Harbor, Maine, also provided valuable guidance. Sarah L. Thomson, an award-winning children's book author, contributed mightily to the daunting project of turning my adult novel *Orphan Train* into one that middle grade students could enjoy. My editor at HarperCollins,

Alexandra Cooper, is smart, kind, and a pure delight to work with. I am grateful for the support of the whole HarperCollins children's division team: Kate Morgan Jackson, associate publisher and editor-in-chief; Rosemary Brosnan, editorial director; Jon Howard, senior production editor; Meaghan Finnerty, senior brand manager; Ann Dye, marketing director; Olivia Russo, publicity manager; David Curtis, designer; Erin Fitzsimmons, associate art director; and Suzanne Murphy, division president. Thanks to my agent, Geri Thoma at Writers House, for shepherding this project through, and to my editor at William Morrow, Katherine Nintzel, for her enormous help with the original manuscript.

This book would not exist without the train riders themselves. Having been privileged to meet eleven of them (all between the ages of ninety and one hundred and two) and read hundreds of their first-person narratives, I am filled with admiration for their courage, fortitude, and perspective on this strange and little-known episode in our nation's history.